as night
follows day

as night follows day

PIERRE MOINOT

TRANSLATED BY
JODY GLADDING
with Elizabeth Deshays

As Night Follows Day by Pierre Moinot

Originally published in France as *Le matin vient et aussi la nuit*.

Copyright © 1999 Editions Gallimard.

Translation © 2001 Welcome Rain Publishers LLC.

Direct any inquiries to

Welcome Rain Publishers LLC, 225 West 35th Street, Suite 1100, New York, NY 10001.

Library of Congress Cataloging-in-Publication Data

Moinot, Pierre

    [Matin vient et aussi la nuit. English]

    As night follows day / Pierre Moinot ; translated by Jody Gladding.

        p. cm.

    ISBN 1-56649-154-1

        I. Gladding, Jody, 1955– II. Title.

    PQ2625.O244M2813 2001

    843'.914—dc21

                                  2001017703

Text design by Cindy LaBreacht

Manufactured in the United States of America by BLAZE I.P.I.

First Edition: June 2001

1 3 5 7 9 10 8 6 4 2

To Elise, Nicolas, Mélanie,
David, Clémentine,
Diégo, and Céleste,
my grandchildren

I thank Bertrand Poirot-Delpech,
who, in his friendly way,
persuaded me to write this book.

Watchman, what of the night?
Morning comes, and also the night.

ISAIAH 20.12

CONTENTS

I

maria

MARIA LEFT THE KITCHEN, holding the two raised corners of her apron in one hand, the brown salad bowl in the other. Where the sun hit a crack in the enamel, a burst of light glinted iridescent, and then, as she approached, went out. With the thick hand of a heavy woman, but with the lightness she must have formerly had, she placed the salad bowl on the table near which Lortier was reading and smoking his pipe. From her apron she poured handfuls of barely downy pea pods, and drew toward her the iron chair, which, raising her eyes, she adjusted so as to avoid the shade of the arbor.

"Your wife tells me that you love these. They're the first ones," she said, "dwarf pods with round peas, very early."

"Where do they come from?" asked Lortier.

"They're yours. I planted them in November."

"So much the better," said Lortier.

It was Mo who especially loved peas so much, like she loved everything, with a consuming pleasure, as if she now wanted to erase the years of deprivation and the mortal anguish of the war, which had only ended two years ago. Since they came from the garden, he would have no choice but to love the peas as well. Absentmindedly he looked out over the valley, the vast lush green meadows where two or three farms had already turned out their animals, the two poplar groves that tapered into grayish pink brushes, the bare fields, their slopes sometimes broken with rocks, pale almond-colored copses still red with the old leaves of the little oaks. Even though it was so vast, and perhaps because the transparent light made everything stand out so clearly, or perhaps because it was so familiar, viewed from the terrace of the old house the entire valley seemed very much alive and peaceful, surprisingly close.

"If I said there was a time when I used to be beautiful," said Maria, "of course no one would believe me."

She split open the first pod with her fingernail, turning it inside out to release the peas with a slight pinging sound.

"And yet, I was beautiful," she began again, "but for a long time I didn't know it, because it was the old women who would catch me by the hair and say to me, 'Look at that, it goes all the way to her butt, look at that color, like wheat.' Even when men said it to me later, it was a small pleasure at first, a warm little mouthful. And what were we? Kids, badly washed, in too-short dresses, with socks and huge shoes too big for us that Madame de Cherves gave my mother, shoes I loved so much because of the heels. After school, when they went there, it's true, we loved to trail along, but with innocent hearts. And I still had that innocent heart, Monsieur, when we began to watch the dancing. When the dance floor was put up on the square on Sunday, there were slits where the tent canvases joined, and of course we didn't have the money to have our palms stamped with the purple stamp that allowed you to come and go as you pleased, the stamp that the bigger girls were so proud of that they tried not to wash it off for a long time to show that their boyfriends had paid for them. Who was going to pay for us, the way we were? When we got tired of watching, we took off our shoes and danced with each other on the grass, near the church.

"It was by opening the slit in the canvas that I saw him for the first time. I didn't know his name was Louis. He danced the waltz like you dance it in the country, completely flat, without any rise, gliding so easily that I imagined him lifted by a string. I saw his profile from the left, then the nape of his neck, then the head of the girl who hid him, then that profile again, the one with the part in his hair, the bridge of his very small nose, a little mustache, a mouth with the lower lip cut in the middle and so red it seemed made up. Maybe I didn't see all that very clearly the first time, but I was caught—I no longer heard the music or the great rumble of heels on the floorboards. I followed the huge circle that all the little turns of the waltz made until the moment when he passed very close to me, those broad shoulders over that girlish waist, the white collar held closed by the black lace of his tie, jacket buttoned nearly all the way up, and that air that seemed so gentle until you noticed his eyes—two icy pupils ringed with yellow like a raptor's, eyes filled with desire—and then you understood that his grace was like the natural agility and suppleness of a sparrow hawk or an eagle or a harrier in flight. When they came to a stop, I let out my breath and I said to Malvina, who was watching with me, 'That's the one I want.' But wait, there was still something else that day, that same day. At the end of the dance, we were there, to watch them all leave, and that man was leaving, too, his arms around the shoulders of two girls who were laughing. He spotted me standing there beside the lifted canvas, and his eyes pierced me as if he were holding me in his talons, all stiff and dressed up and maybe even dirty with my long braid hanging to my butt. He let go of the girls. He pointed with his index finger, which he placed, very lightly, on my forehead, without saying a word, staring at me almost harshly, looking me up and down, his eyes prying through me, and his face had become the face of a hunter who discovers a hare in its den. I stood frozen; I did not even realize that I tried to take his hand to kiss it. Then he broke into laughter and said to me, 'Are you crazy? Wait to grow up a bit, little marvel!' He left, but he said that, those words exactly. From that night on, I carried myself gloriously."

Maria fell silent without interrupting her work, sometimes carefully putting aside an opened pod in which the small white larva of a pea weevil wriggled about. Lortier filled his pipe with his index finger, taking little puffs, all the time regarding the valley, which late April's rising light seemed to flatten out, and then Maria, lost in distant thoughts that the automatic gestures of her task accompanied.

Lortier asked, "How old were you?"

"Ah," said Maria, "how old? Twelve, thirteen, I think. I had already finished grade school. I don't really know what happened there. I read a lot, everything, everything that fell into my hands, all the books in the local library. The teacher wanted me to go on for my diploma because I was a quick learner, but my mother said that wasn't possible for us. I worked as a shepherdess at Udron, a big farm; it seems to me I had more than thirty goats. No doubt I had forgotten that man and the slit in the tent and his finger on my forehead. I knew some boys, I had my fun with them, but it was like a game, and when you stopped playing, there wasn't anything more, each of you found you were all alone again with your work.

Then I took my mother's place at old Madame de Cherves's, whom we called the marchioness, though I don't believe she was one, seeing as I myself called her Madame. I was not a chambermaid, no, just a regular servant, except that in my case, young Monsieur de Cherves never touched me. Yes, I carried myself gloriously," she said, as if that formula had captivated her with its accuracy, "but Monsieur René never touched me, maybe because I intimidated him, because despite my years I had retained a childlike newness, my skin breathed something intact, yes, a pure freshness, so that whenever I caught a glimpse of my face in a mirror I was amazed at seeing how much the body lies, never keeping up with life very well, and the other way around, too, I tell myself, at the age I've reached now. Still it's true that Monsieur René, who was red-faced and as strong as a Turk, did try to kiss me once and that was all. He had plenty enough to do to look after his wife."

"I knew them all," said Lortier, "old Méhus de Cherves and the marchioness, and René and beautiful Nedège. Knew them from a distance."

Maria barely smiled, perhaps because Lortier did nothing but look out over the valley as he listened. Or perhaps the smile was only at the memory of those he had named.

"Beautiful Nedège," she repeated. "I would be lying if I said that Madame René wasn't beautiful, her hair as dark as mine was blond, but cut short, with pale forget-me-not blue eyes. Bold, well filled out, heartless, the money running through her fingers, and cold, it seemed to us, since we knew that René often knocked on her bedroom door without her opening it, until we happened upon certain comings and goings. Madame didn't like her, Nedège, oh yes, she detested her, but with so much politeness, such icy kindness, that the other one could never say anything, only feel that she was detested. Still, it was in the midst of the entangled feelings of all these people that I learned to live in a different way, without great pleasure or distaste, and I did grow up, as he had said, and I was as much my own mistress as you please when I wanted to be. Then Louis came back, and there, too, I did just exactly what I wanted."

She raised her eyes, moistened her lips with her tongue, glanced quickly over the valley, then toward Lortier, and continued.

"He remembered a long time after that first day. He had served on the ships in Rochefort, and then he took a job as a sailor on the yachts, and maybe it was the sea that had softened his look, because he still had that sparrow hawk eagerness, but sometimes it all melted away as if he became a sort of submissive child, happy to obey that great hunger that came over him. From the moment he saw me, it was as if I had been magnetized. He came right to me and without a word we danced the first dance, then all the others, hardly talking. I felt so strange that my astonishment at being in such a state occupied me almost more than what aroused me. I was overcome with the sudden closeness of this man, with his scent, his hands as they held me, his strength and lightness, his face, which sometimes touched mine. And something in me looked upon this madness and smiled at the desire I had for him, something discovered that all I had to do was wait and rejoice in my victory. From that moment on, I knew I would give in only when I had decided, but that was a small detail, because the part of me that was watching myself suddenly saw everything like you see a plain from high up in a tree, and I knew exactly what was in store for me there:

great happiness and great suffering, as children must offer you over the years, a being who would never leave me, without ever ceasing to flee, and whom I would always dominate, when all was said and done, without ever being able to hold."

Maria fell silent, placed the salad bowl, which had grown heavy as she held it between her knees, onto the table, gathered a few empty fallen pods from the ground, and put them with the others, which she carefully made into a pile. Lortier secretly glanced at her. She was dreaming. Here was an ageless woman, whose stoutness had smoothed out her cheeks but hadn't been able to erase the deep folds that saddened her colorless mouth or the network of wrinkles and nearly black shadows around her eyes. Her face's normal expression was attentive, sometimes lightly marked with worry. From the youth that revisited this morning, she had retained a kind of greenness as changeable as that of a willow leaf, and an enormous head of hair, now short and white, but so thick and heavy it seemed to lighten and thin her features, a disproportionate halo from which a few strands of gold still gleamed. Her hands, which she held one in the other, fluttered faintly a few times, and then distractedly her left hand picked up a full pod, which her right hand opened. Mechanically, her vacant eyes watched what her hands did. Lortier restrained himself from questioning her, and indeed, she took up her story again.

"I quickly realized this man was a weak and unfaithful creature. Only his appeal was so delightfully overpowering that he regained all he lost, lost precisely because of that very power. At least he thought so, because as for me, I didn't care a bit about his escapades, the hairs that I found on his jacket, occasional letters forgotten in a pocket, first names carelessly uttered or shirts half buttoned maybe because some husband had arrived too soon. I didn't care one bit, but I kept watch. He worked for a grain merchant, in Beloux. He was all muscle, he could carry a sack of wheat all by himself on one shoulder, he did pickups and deliveries for the farms and mills, sometimes he left less quickly than he'd gone in, often I knew where. Maybe the effect that had on me, that stone, there, in my chest, maybe that was jealousy after all. But never a word. I would have gotten nothing but cajoling from him; he did not know how to hide what he tried to win forgiveness for. And maybe I never, never forgave anything, but what he knew how to do to my body and what bound me to him beyond the body was stronger than everything else. He entered by the little door at the end of the grounds with the key that I'd gotten copied. I oiled its hinges so it wouldn't squeak. He only had to go around by the boxwood path, passing behind the greenhouse, and no one could see him from the house. My room was just at the end, in a little outbuilding attached to the kitchen, which I shared with old Jamine, the cook, who really made fun of what I did, deaf though she was. Depending on the day, it was raging passion, or a frightening slowness, or a sharp and joyous pleasure. I followed after him in everything he desired, in everything he wanted to teach me, and sometimes I was so impassioned I invented things on my own. He directed and dominated my pleasure, but at the same time he was slave to it, since his depended upon mine just as completely as water needs a slope to run down. And sometimes our pleasure was so ethereal that it didn't seem to me to come from our bodies. I advanced into a huge, dazzling, virgin country, I entered somewhere else, I don't know where. Or sometimes Louis led me into deep underground passageways, coarse, muddy ways that glistened darkly, that fascinated me, and I was terrified and overjoyed by those brutal words that possessed me, and which became beautiful themselves as well, naked and raw, as if love had washed them clean.

"I was in a poor little room with only a sorry armoire for my things, a small night table, a washstand with basin and pitcher, and nothing on the walls but a crucifix and his boxwood branch over the bed, but that might have been where I was the happiest in all my life. You are going to say that I'm blasphemous, Monsieur, but since I'm telling everything, I might as well say this as well: even though my mother had raised me in her religion, I never practiced much except to please Madame de Cherves, but in those moments when I was carried out of myself by Louis, into the light of the infinite, or the darkness, I don't know, I sometimes looked up at the crucifix as if my body were nothing other than an immense prayer, yes, that was what I experienced at that moment, all that I was gave thanks. May God forgive me."

She had suddenly spoken louder and with greater animation. She stopped for a moment, then began again more softly in her usual voice, rough from wine and tobacco.

"He slept like a baby. I watched all the little bubbles of saliva that formed and broke on his lips as he breathed. I listened to his breathing. I caressed his neck, his shoulder without him feeling, I told him that I loved him without him hearing. I was joined to this man without being blind to either my pride or his weakness. I knew moments when together we formed only a single being, whether it was in our pleasure and thanks to it, or often in a way foreign to pleasure, which alone was enough for me, which belonged to me alone. And I cannot call that anything but love, but it was not so for him. He could not love as I loved. Sometimes I believed that he rose higher and that he was going to join me, but he didn't know how to get beyond his pleasure. And maybe that was exactly what he sought, without being aware of it, in that desire he had for change, for trying other women. At least that's what I told myself for a while, because I never did understand that his greatest pleasure was only in seduction. Only that."

She fell silent, pushed the open pods into the pile with the back of her hand, rested and looked out on the valley. Lortier smoked but no longer swung back in his chair. He sat upright with an elbow on the table and slowly drew on his pipe, watching Maria. He was stunned and fascinated. Everyone in the village knew Maria, though she wasn't a prominent figure because she kept to her place and wasn't a gossip. She was a servant at Madame Papot's, in the part of the village called the Bastière, which was nearly all Protestant, and three times a week she came to Puypouzin for a few hours to help Mo with the housework or to help him, Lortier, with the garden, or especially to help with the cooking, for which she had a great gift. When by chance it came up in conversation, her story was kept to three sentences, with the omission of only one time in her life that no one knew anything about, except that she had lived in La Rochelle or Rochefort, which no one knew how or why. Lortier liked Maria very much: even though she was quite heavy, she was quick and determined, she spoke little but in an open and easy way, and she wasn't by nature envious, but inclined, on the contrary, to be helpful and lend a hand. These general traits were enough up until then to justify the sympathy he felt toward her, the friendly exchanges of small talk, and her pleasant way of commenting on village news. But the account that she had decided to give that morning was of a different kind, and the willingness with which she gave it had a meaning he still didn't understand. He only knew that he must ask no questions. He picked up a few peas and began to shell them, and Maria pushed the salad bowl toward him.

"The memory," she said, "is like those old aqueducts. Everything that is too heavy to be carried along falls to the bottom, the rest slips along with life. I thought I was very vigilant at that time; I forgot that jealousy falls asleep in the drowsiness of love. Louis had to come deliver barley for the horses just at the moment when she was in the stable yard saddling her mare. And it was in her riding clothes that she might have been the most beautiful, with those boots and that very tight-waisted jacket, opened over the lace of her blouse. I can still imagine Louis's eyes, and she who had such great need for a tender man. At first, I neither saw nor knew anything, except that on certain evenings he arrived much later or didn't come at all, because he had been delivering sacks that were too heavy too far away. I don't know what alerted me, maybe in the middle of the night the very vague feeling that something of him escaped me, and then, a long time afterward, I was struck one night by a certain perfume that still clung to his skin and that I immediately recognized, just as if that perfume had cried out the name of the woman who had pressed herself against him hard enough for her scent to be delivered to me without fail. Beginning that night, I watched Madame René. I had been foolish enough not to see that she was much more cheerful, much kinder to her husband, that her outings were much

longer, that she wore more perfume, that idiot, without the slight-
est idea that she was betraying herself. Then the outings returned to
their normal length and I realized that the meeting places must have
changed. I kept careful watch, I spied. I happened to notice that the
door to the greenhouse wasn't closed right, and I saw that she, too,
had been oiling it. What we called the greenhouse was just a big conservatory from which we had already taken the cane plants, the
geraniums, the two lemon trees, the lantana, and the gardenias,
which Madame was so attached to, anything that might be hurt by
frost. All that was left in there were tools and pots, a cupboard of little drawers for seeds, and a wall of bags of compost behind which I
found their niche on the straw matting: a big pile of old jute sacks
and thick carriage covers that were no longer used.

"Maybe our nature is not as bad as it seems, even though in that
one instant I was filled with very violent feelings, hatred, anger, dis-
gust, scorn, revenge, and others no doubt more base than those. I did
not know right away that those savage thoughts expressed nothing
other than love, that they were its refuse, so to speak, its excrement,
that they were proof of its strength and life. I mounted guard. Twice,
about eleven o'clock at night—I had already helped Madame to bed,
Monsieur René, who got up every morning at five, was asleep, I was
hidden in the boxwood arbor—I saw her go out by the French windows, in her dressing gown, and walk peacefully back and forth as if
she had come out for the fresh night air in the moonlight, and then
this little walk very gradually led toward the greenhouse, where
Louis surely was already waiting. I had discovered their signal, a red
rag hidden under a stone at the bottom end of the grounds, which
she hung on one of the points of the little gate. When the rag was on

the gate, Louis slipped along the boxwood as if to come to my room, but he turned in at the greenhouse and hid there. I knew him well enough to be sure that this moment of waiting was undoubtedly the most pleasurable one for him, when he could imagine everything, and maybe he was even pleased at having the mistress after having had the servant. And her, I knew just by looking at her, she was made to do the taking without knowing how to give. And I could have watched them, but I didn't want to know what kind of lover she was, oh no! Never that!

"I could have ruined that house. But I was not driven by such arrogance. If I had let slip at the right time a few small suspicions, Madame would have been only too happy. She would have set her schemes in motion as only she knew how to do, and poor Monsieur René would have found himself obliged to decide, to yell, to punish, everything he hated most in the world. I didn't like such roundabout methods. This was just between her and me, even though she didn't know she'd taken what was mine, but she had taken it. I wanted to humiliate her. The night I saw the red rag hanging, after my duties I stood watch in the boxwood. I saw Louis edge his way into the greenhouse, the lights in the house went out, I saw her come out quickly without even making the pretense of a little walk, and she was not even at the glass door before she had her dressing gown off. The moon was full, the conservatory was lit by a very white light, which its green walls turned matte, and I saw her come forward undressed like a kind of ghost, and then she disappeared behind the sacks. Maybe I was jealous of the bravery in her desire or her ignorance of me. I had the goodness to wait a moment, and then I made myself entirely naked, I undid my braid and freed my hair, which enclosed me like fabric, almost gray in that moonlight. I crossed the conservatory. I found them lying down. I put my foot on her. She gave a little cry. There she was extended before me, the beautiful Nedège de Cherves, naked as I was yet more terror-stricken by my nakedness than her own. And Louis was pinned down by fear, as if I were an apparition. She sat up, her arms across her breasts, she raised her terrified eyes toward me. She didn't understand why I was there or why I was naked. Then I said, "This is my place. Get out." I said it in a very quiet voice, with no anger, looking at Louis, and immediately, she disappeared. I lay down next to that weak man and that night I was, in the true sense of the word, his mistress. I talk too much, Monsieur, I talk too much."

"You have trusted me with a great confidence, Maria."

"Would you permit me to smoke? I need a cigarette."

Lortier offered his tobacco pouch, but she refused and pulled out from a pocket, under her skirt, a packet of gray tobacco and a book of papers from which she detached a sheet with her fingernail. While she rolled her cigarette, Lortier rose, walked to the kitchen, and returned with a bottle of wine and two glasses, which he filled, and then held out his lighter for Maria. They clinked glasses.

"Madame Papot doesn't know that I smoke," said Maria.

"And afterward," said Lortier, "what happened?"

She drank two big, thirsty swallows, wiped her lips, and gave a little fatalistic shrug of her shoulders.

"That hardly matters, you know. I stayed with Madame for a week. When I crossed paths with that woman, my eyes did not look at her, we didn't say a word to each other. I married Louis. We left for La Palice, where he found a job at the port unloading wood from the colonies. We rented a little house in Aigrefeuille and I worked for two old maiden ladies, one was a piano teacher, the other played the violin. Hoisting those enormous blocks of mahogany and nyangon, Louis started drinking, first at work, and then even at home. And little by little, I drank, too. In a few years, he had lost his seductive charm, he had become a strong and brutal man who lived in regret. His only remaining power was that brute strength, and he used it on me for the lack of anything better. Gradually, through hating women, he became nearly wild. It was as if he were taking revenge, on them, on me, on himself, I don't know. I was only allowed to polish or to wash what he owned, which is to say everything, since I had nothing. He could no longer stand it if I kissed him. He couldn't stand it if at the grocer's I was called Madame Louis. He screamed that I was a slut, that he'd picked me out of the gutter. He was like a slow torturer, he needed to debase me, starve me. He ate alone, and I had to stand there in front of him. We had become poor. When the maiden ladies cooked something special, they often gave me a part of it, and I brought it home to him, or when there was asparagus, and the ladies only ate the tips, I made up the rest for him in a béchamel sauce. I cared for him like a child despite his brutalities and his insults because he was not happy. Once, however, I surprised him by remembering how, one day, it had been windy and sunny, my hat had blown off, and in the effort I'd made to catch it, my bun had come undone and my hair had streamed all the way down my back like a fox's pelt. It was just a small moment that I had forgotten, but for him, in recalling it, all his harshness and violence disappeared in a single stroke, and he smiled like in the old days.

"As for me, my happiness was all in the music those ladies played. I stayed to listen to them after my working hours without Louis knowing it, because he would have beaten me because of the housework that wasn't done. That music made me cry and consoled me at the same time. I told myself that I had become the old woman of a second-rate man, but when I thought about the way I had loved, I believed that nothing and no one could take that treasure away from me."

"You have just given it to me," said Lortier.

He wanted to fill her glass again, but she refused with a gesture of her hand and took out her tobacco.

"From the time I came here, I recognized the way you live, your wife and you," she said as she rolled her cigarette. "Sometimes to see you two together does the same thing to me as the music used to. Watching you, I still feel pride at having been so deeply within a man's heart, or maybe only within my own. Touching upon it does me harm, it destroys me. Madame Papot is very good all in all, but no doubt she imagines that the life I led before coming to her was dark and reprehensible, and that sets her teeth on edge. And it's true, in one sense. Louis is dead because he had to drink and he didn't see that big block of mahogany the crane operator was lifting. But once he was dead, I could embrace him to my heart's content. Those ladies kept me on, but finally I couldn't stand their pity. For a long time, I fell into what you'd have to call hard times. And in the end, I returned to this village as an old servant. Now you know that the way in which I loved Louis is what has remained most pure in my life. We will never speak of it again, if you wouldn't mind."

"Never again," said Lortier.

II

adrien

WHILE HE UNTIED THE GOATS, Adrien leaned over the little kid whom he secretly kissed on the muzzle and in that soft hollow of the head, telling him very quietly to be good. Then he took his stick and ran to take his place in front of the gate to the road, through which the herd would go out. Sirène, the dog, was waiting there. The cows whom Fernand had untied crossed the yard walking calmly or snorting, according to their nature, and stopped out of habit before the old stone sarcophagus, which was used as a sink, sniffing the water, some of them dipping their muzzles in for a moment but more anxious to be going than to drink. Adrien knew all six of them by name, but the goats were referred to as the mother, the pig, the three little ones, and the mule. He looked happily over the yard from which he was escaping. Fernand called out that he ought to have them drink at the stream coming back, to save the well water, and Adrien—pack on his back, with short trousers, his socks falling down over his large clogs, an old sweater much too big for him covering most of his hands—sang out a long yes of pleasure before opening the gate and looking out over the road.

Behind his almost too-anxious herd, he took the bend that led away from the part of the village called the Guérinière, followed the road for a moment, and then took up a path beaten flat by the animals' feet, which led down to the valley meadows. The cows were all of the Parthenaise breed, with fawn-colored coats and no spots. Those were the conditions set by the Echiré cooperative, which took away the milk collected each morning in an old gas-fired truck. Without worrying too much about their guardian, whose young age they seemed to have weighed, they stopped where the path narrowed to greedily devour a few tufts of green grass standing out against the gray of the embankment. Judging this fault not too serious, Sirène intervened only if Adrien asked her to, and without much insistence. Adrien didn't like either to yell or to hit, even though he was afraid of not being able to make himself be obeyed, and sometimes his responsibility for the herd made his throat feel tight. Then he threatened with his stick, or jabbed it into a flank or a leg. If it was necessary to strike after all, he took care to avoid the back, where the bones ran under the skin, and he rapped on the fat of the thigh. And perhaps he was sparing with his blows because according to a deal he had made with himself, he was obliged to answer for them by beating himself on the behind, or the thighs, or sometimes the shoulders with his stick, when there was no risk of the contortions that punishment required being seen.

Halfway down the hill, under the canopy of ash hiding the valley, he heard another herd behind him, slowed his pace, and recognized Albert Mainson's cow with the closed horns in the lead. Over the heads of the beasts he was just ahead of, he called to Albert, who also had seen him.

"Where are you going?" cried Albert. "Into the Noue?"

"No, I have to go up, to Champarnaud. Is Alice coming?"

"So you won't be with us? You can't come down to see us?"

"No, it's too far."

"Alice must be in front of us. Her yard was wide open. So you won't come? What have you learned for tomorrow?"

"The prepositions and Du Guesclin."

"Oh my!"

Adrien waved his stick good-bye and ran to get ahead of his herd, which had just reached the entrance to the path leading to the Noue, and turned them toward Champarnaud. He would not see Alice today. He listened to Albert turn off and then returned to just the noise of his animals, his own steps, the panting of his dog; and all at once, after a fleeting regret, he entered into the happiness of being alone. The cows had understood where he was leading them and hurried along now. They crossed the stream at Pont-Bertrand, disdaining the washing place where they normally drank, and soon took a narrow path that climbed straight up the other side of the valley and seemed even steeper because of the branches of the elms just leafing out to form a tunnel over it. After a moment, followed by the hurrying backs of the goats, they entered the field, where the two younger ones began to frisk and run while Adrien closed the gate again behind him.

Adrien was small despite his twelve years, with very black curly hair, so black it was almost blue, and pale eyes so luminous that just seeing them was enough to bring back a time of innocence. Everything was still mingled in him, along with shadows that he himself didn't know about. He was bright and a dreamer, emotional and wild, straightforward but reticent, starved for affection, and sometimes, deep within and all alone, overcome by an inordinate violence, which he kept hidden. Dreams and gentleness alone could be read on the oval of that face, as solemn as those of the angel musicians in ancient paintings. Everything else remained dormant beneath this restrained air.

He was hot after the climb. He calmly took his place under the old ash, where a big rock was still surrounded by walls of russet moss out of which, last time, he had fashioned a house and door, like those military blueprints in his books, or like the remains of a very ancient ruin that some excavation might have brought to light. He entered by the door, scolded the dog who was knocking down a piece of moss, and undid his sack, from which he chose those among his schoolbooks that were from the library: the red cover of *Twenty Thousand Leagues Under the Sea,* and the green cover of *White Fang,* which he placed on the rock. He had time to read; this long solitary afternoon was his own domain, in which even the moments of boredom belonged to him.

First he gazed at Champarnaud, its very gentle slope softening and rounding the heights of steep stubble fields. Above, toward the north, a high hedge hid the Outremont plain and spread out, on the other side of the gate, into a thick little woods from which rose ash trees, twisted and stunted by the dry years. To the south, a short hedge of thorns and brambles, hardly higher than a drystone wall, allowed for a long view of the other side of the valley, toward the oblique fields and groves, then beyond them to an endless plain divided up into colors where the green of winter wheat dominated, and the radiant yellow of rapeseed. This checkerboard was studded with dark cypress marking the graveyards of Protestant families in certain corners of the fields. At the distant horizon, the plain was no more than a blue line, but Adrien knew that beyond this line extended still other plains, and villages and cities grew up there. He knew that behind it there was a whole map, an entire world where he might someday go, and the promise of that vastness made him smile happily.

His mind full of hazy daydreams, he stood lost for a long time, contemplating unknown countries. He tried to imagine the cities. He constructed houses side by side, with neither yard nor stable, closely lining a road, from which emerged many people in the midst of whom he was running about without even greeting them. The houses changed according to his wish, the people grew or shrank, or suddenly froze in place. And behind these cities Adrien made forests grow, inhabited with prehistoric animals, mountains with snow-capped peaks or spitting fire, enormous waterfalls similar to the torrents that poured endlessly in the picture of the "Wonders of the World" glued onto the cover of his class notebook. All these places, and others momentarily glimpsed, visited in dreams, or fixed for good by the illustrations in his books and crossed by the wanderings of hunters, bandits, savages, heroes. Finally he entered into huge tumultuous waves like those that lifted up the *Tankadère* in *Around the World in Eighty Days,* and then into a blue and flat expanse into which the *Nautilus* sank, both of which were the sea.

He was transported by the power of this invention until the distant song of a cuckoo brought him back to the Outremont, onto that great plain of meadows or the fields behind it, and then to the very place where he was, suddenly so present that it surprised him. The invisible deceitful cuckoo drew closer now, prolonging its cry with a third syllable, which meant he was seeking a mate. In the woods, the blackbirds' raucous whistling exploded joyously each time they shot out of the thickets in intersecting streaks to the tufts of the ash, where their erratic game chased off a thrush, whose melody blended with the flute of the warblers two trees away. Adrien listened to the confused arabesques of their songs, their uninterrupted music of endlessly changing scores played for themselves alone and offered freely, regardless of who heard them. And the woods rippled with intense activity, for which these songs were only the echo. He listened. The flight of a hoopoe unwound its name as it trailed off, while the cuckoo approached. Nearly at the same time, Adrien came upon those flowers born and baptized sisters by the cry of the bird, their yellow calyxes hugging the corners of the wall and the woods. He ran toward them, stumbling over a wide arc of sweet-smelling violets. He stopped short in front of the very low entrance of the passage to his hiding place, under the thicket; in a blue shadow, a patch of leaning wood hyacinths, which he called bellflowers, extended far into the woods. These discoveries, mingled with the incessant chirping of birds, with the fertile stillness of that immense plain over there reaching to the horizon, suddenly filled Adrien with measureless joy. He trembled with excitement, as if enchanted by the mixed charms of the teeming reality he heard and saw, and the imagined and changing forms over which he ruled. The cows grazed peacefully, the goats had quieted down, all in keeping with a secret holiday in which he shared. Taken by some unknown exaltation, he ran this way and that, rolled in the grass, bit it off in pleasure, felt himself being led he didn't know where, radiant with what seemed to him both water and thirst, while Sirène, either nervous about these fits or seized by them herself, danced around him, barking. His chest wasn't large enough for the breath that such great discoveries demanded. He would have liked to contain them, to swallow them, to drink them—he would have liked to shout for joy. He got to his feet laughing to rush upon Sirène and gather her in his arms to kiss her.

He was curled up in the dog's warm fur, no longer thinking of anything, listening to a kind of ecstasy slowly settle down in him and gradually return to serenity, bringing everything dancing and bewitching back to the modest rank they'd held before his rapture had magnified them. This return was not bitter; it lasted a long time, it wrapped everything in a great sweetness, under the good and indulgent eye of the cows.

He lay on the ground, chased away the dog who kept licking his face. The tumult that had just overcome him and that had gradually subsided left him. The scythe stroke of a swallow's flight sliced through the transparent sky, nearly white in its blueness. In the vast plain called Beauce, Zacharie had told him, the wells were so deep that when they agreed to clean them out, the well workers saw the huge sky overhead like a ten-sou piece, but they could see the stars in broad daylight. With his two closed fists, Adrien made a spyglass, its end as small as a well. Not a single star appeared. The name of Zacharie evoked the odor of wood shavings; the image of his workshop in the Bastière led to the neighboring farm of Simon Varadier, called Malidure, since everyone in the village was referred to by what they called a coname. There Alice lived, "your girlfriend, your sweetheart," Morisson had said in the boys' schoolyard, and Adrien had not known if he should be proud of that or blush.

It was very difficult for him to establish preferences among those he loved, because he didn't love them all in the same way.

Definitely the first was Maria, who covered him with kisses, who secretly prepared pastry cones for him with plums or dried figs. When she took him in her arms, a very ancient warmth flowed through him, which he seemed to recognize as an indecipherable memory from another time. All that was soft and dark with Maria was radiant and mysterious with Alice. Alice was eleven years old, a year younger than him. After school, she often kept her head lowered next to him, as if he weren't there, then suddenly raised her little pointed face with hungry eyes and plunged into his gaze as if she had planted a knife. In the Noue, they found themselves with Albert Mainson, Rosa Mousset, sometimes Edmond—the oldest, who already had his diploma—but they often played alone, he and Alice, telling each other stories. Out of red wild rose hips, he carved her little hanging baskets, shaping the handles so that they could slide through her earlobes. When the others couldn't see them, he sometimes dared to kiss her. She didn't say anything, her eyes widened, and so close to this angelic white face, Adrien couldn't see anything but those enormous eyes, purple as a crocus. Alice was sweet, and perhaps sweeter still was the memory of Alice mixed with a kind of new promise that mingled this memory with expectation. The way in which he loved Clémence, whom he called Maman, was not the least bit like that. Clémence was his good guardian, at his bedside through his childhood illnesses, taking care of his clothes and food, even though more and more often, after doing the work Fernand left undone because of his drinking, her exhaustion made her attention for him lapse completely. At those times he was alone, accompanied from a distance by a too-tired shadow who renounced her protective maternal role. He knew that Clémence was profoundly good but that nothing had prepared her for tenderness. She kissed him on the forehead at night, and perhaps because this kiss was the only one, he waited for it and struggled to stay awake until he received it.

Fernand and Adrien's teacher belonged to another category. Away from the bottle, sober, Fernand knew many things, which he talked about in a lively and even cheerful way. He was a very good farmer, who loved to instruct Adrien in his occupation, who also attached primary importance to school and grades, who looked over Adrien's workbooks. Adrien called him "my father." This happy bond was broken as soon as Fernand gave way to wine, which led him indiscriminately into a great confusion of gestures or talk, into violence, into a fog of drowsiness and oblivion, sometimes into the bitterness of laughter. If he happened to take it out on the child at these times, Clémence always intervened, except once, and as she was big and strong and determined, Fernand gave in before seeking refuge in the cellar. As for the teacher, because Adrien was a good student, he paid particular attention to him, taking great care that Adrien's classmates observed no special treatment. Between Adrien and himself there was a spiritual bond, which inhered in feelings and attitudes, an unspoken predilection but so rich an exchange that school was always a happy place.

Very far off, there were loud, sometimes regular noises, like gunshots. No doubt it was Jeandet who was driving chestnut stakes with a sledgehammer to hold in the bulging stream wall at the great bend. Sometimes the echo merged with the original. Dreaming, Adrien made a world tour. He told himself that on the one side, he put tenderness and protection, which served him as a roof, and on the other, something like law. He had forgotten Sirène and his friend the little kid goat, so gentle that he did not let himself be cajoled. Completely apart, he set Monsieur and Madame Lortier, to whom he often delivered milk. Lortier had given him the only treasure he possessed, his knife with the Swiss cross and chain for attaching to a button, in exchange for a big flint in the shape of an almond. Previously he broke the flints that he found so that upon impact he could breathe in the smell of a thunderstorm. Lortier had taught him what certain ones were, how to recognize them, and each time that he brought him one, he was given a coin, even if he found them again later tossed onto a small rock pile close to the entrance. Often Madame Lortier asked Maria to make chocolate mousse for him. She had taken his measurements to knit him a sweater, and once for his birthday, she had bought him a beautiful shirt. On the walls there were pictures drawn in black of large landscapes and other paintings, the one he liked best representing fruits and game. Puypouzin was not entirely a place for country people, but he was received there as if he were arriving back home after a long absence.

The echo sent two sharp blows, spaced apart, from Jeandet toward the plain, and then restored a regular hammering to the stream. The animals had not eaten their fill, but they were well behaved, even the goats who methodically stripped the lower branches of the little elms. Adrien got up, took his bread and a beautiful apple, all wrinkled, from his lunch bag, told Sirène that he was entrusting the herd to her, and crawled on his hands and knees into the nearly invisible entrance of the narrow tunnel that pierced the thicket. Later, he must make two bouquets: one of bellflowers, which he would gather without uprooting for Maria, one of violets, which he would tie with a piece of grass for Clémence. He wouldn't see Alice—if she had been there, they would have been able to put the cuckoo's yellow wood narcissus very close together on a string long enough to knot and wind up into a ball they could play with. For the moment, he had to visit his hiding place.

It was intact. Biting into his apple, he inspected this shelter in the form of a big egg in which he could really only squat or sit on a thick bed of dead leaves that were still a little damp. Cutting them with his knife or intertwining the branches of hazel, privet, and wild daphne, he had hollowed out this place in the thickness of the undergrowth, baptized castaway refuge, pirate-ship deck, or smugglers' cave, according to the time and day. Most of the time, it was Robinson Crusoe's besieged encampment, in which he now checked where all the muskets were, and the ammunition that consisted of a collection of oak galls gathered from the oaks and arranged on a stone plate. The stock of provisions under an arum leaf was all there: old hazelnuts, sloe berries, and white mushrooms, to which he added a small square cut from his apple. He could also resist the German counterattack in this small fort, taking up no longer the musket but the tommy gun and savagely mowing down all comers, touching them right on the chest and knocking them over, scattering their weapons and grenades, their arms flung open wide as they fell. It was a slaughter. Then he slipped imperceptibly from the state of lone survivor to dispenser of justice, and became Robin Hood in the Sherwood Forest.

Just as the avenging arrow left his bow, the noise of running coming closer, above the woods, instantly brought the game to an end. He heard the footsteps, more and more distinct, the panting of the runner who was no doubt following along the hedge above, stopping, forcing his way into the woods with the loud noise of branches. Frozen with fear, Adrien saw a vague silhouette that dropped to its knees, scratched in the rustling dead leaves, then seemed to make a pile of them, then stood up again to charge out of the woods and take off running. Adrien's curiosity was stronger than his fear. You didn't run in the village without some urgent reason, and almost without thinking about it, he wanted to know who was running. He rushed out of his hiding place, pushed away Sirène, who leaped about in greeting, jumped onto the corner of the wall, cleared the low hedge behind it with his two feet together, and threw himself onto the little trail that the badgers had traced in the high stubble. If the runner was going to the village, he had no choice: he would pass by the foot of the big wall surrounding the terrace at Puypouzin, cross the lower bridge, and take the stone path that climbed from the bridge diagonally to rejoin the road between the last houses. Adrien jumped over two walls that badgers or foxes had toppled, crossed the tongue of thicket descending there to the meadows, ran for a long time, slowed down when Puypouzin's high wall and rock appeared, and kneeled behind the last stubble field border. His heart hammered. He didn't know if the runner had already passed or if he was going to spring out of the woods, which descended nearly to the terrace door fifty meters away from him. But the runner had been faster; Adrien saw him from the back climbing the stone path, hatless, dressed in a brown hunting jacket that puffed out on the sides, walking at a quick pace interspersed with little runs on the very steep slope. It seemed to him that he recognized this silhouette, but it was only a fleeting sensation, too vague to be sure of, and it vanished as the man grew smaller in the distance. Adrien moved slightly and saw in a line the man, the place where the path joined the road, and the fish seller's car, which was still running and was stopped at this crossroads to serve clients in the last houses. Suddenly the figure darted from the path and turned off. Adrien searched for him at the edge of the rabbit warren, where he blended with the color of the thicket and could only be seen by his movement. The man followed the edge of the woods, jumped into the embankment of a little path that led down from the gardens behind the houses, and disappeared.

Adrien looked all around him: undoubtedly no one had seen what he had witnessed there, and he himself didn't know why the man was running. Then he remembered the herd that he had abandoned, and the seriousness of his crime made him freeze. As quickly as he could, he went back to Champarnaud. The little hedge reinforcing the wall, uncrossable from this side, made it necessary for him to take the gate, where Sirène was already waiting for him. All was calm. He counted the goats, caught his breath, thanked Sirène with a caress, and found the moss house and his rock again with his pack and books. He had no more desire to play. It seemed to him that he had just brushed up against a mystery foreign to his own world. But maybe this wasn't a mystery, there were many reasons that might require grown-ups to run. But not to rush into the woods and shuffle the leaves around. He was afraid of going to see that spot now, although he had to. He reentered his hiding place, where the rest of his apple was waiting, took off his sweater, which could get caught on anything, and started off on hands and knees through the thicket, nervous and proud at the same time, aware that this was a real expedition. Clutching his stick, which he dragged along beside him like a weapon, he struck the leaves and ivy in front of him every once in a while to scare away snakes, whom he hated. Finally he reached the hollow of the slope marking the end of the woods, a dark embankment over which the edge of the fields on the plain shone light and open. He saw a long heap of dead leaves, kneeled down, and pushed them away with his stick, then with his hands. Suddenly in a tumult, his youthful levity vanished, snatched away by the hard world of men where the plains ended, without birds or hiding places—at that moment when he drew his hand back quickly, surprised and nearly injured by the cold steel, his hand frozen by this sacrilegious discovery, which made it necessary for him to touch once more the irreparable reality of a gleaming steel gun barrel: to recognize it, to cover it back up again, to carefully rebuild the leaf pile just as he had found it.

lortier

CARRYING HIS SMALL WOODEN TUB, Hubert Lortier went out in the evening to the end of the terrace and through the little door that opened into the valley, cut across the path heading down to the lower bridge, took a few steps along the little road, and turned around, as he always did, to look at the house. It was massive, strong, and very old, covered with a great Roman tile roof except for the tower, where on the stationary mercury of the slates the light shifted with each passing cloud. Built on the rocky spot where the stubble fields ended, it looked out over the countryside and protected itself, still threatening the lower bridge with a few loopholes, while a thick wall in back defended rear access by the plateau. As a child, when he watched the cows during his vacation, like little Adrien did, he never passed by the walled house—which seemed to him like a cliff as primitive as the rock—without imagining old battles, sieges, departures, an ancient and dormant past for which it remained the witness, as if the farm it had become, despite centuries of deterioration and change, still remotely resembled the stronghold it must have originally been. Above the back gate, in the north wall, he remembered there was a little lodging with a nearly collapsed roof, a long and very low room that must have provided shelter for the peasant lookouts, and in which old

Baudou, called Roquet, called Griffeécus, raised rabbits. Lortier remembered this hard man, stooped, distrustful, who gave old long-handled razors to his wife in place of knives. For fear that someone would switch the oak planks he had put aside for pine, he had his coffin made with a padlock and stored his potatoes there. Each evening, his daughter had to ask him for some for the soup. He watched her like milk set on a stove to warm. But that didn't prevent the Monéteau boy—after looks and notes exchanged in the hymnals during mass, and backed up by the saying that a suitor is more cunning than a thief—from forcing his way in, with the complicity of the mother, who finally saw some good fortune entering the house.

But returning from market, the old man discovered three eggshells in the fireplace instead of two. He redoubled his guard, barred the doors, and secured the locks—so well that Marie, the daughter, shut away, fed on bread and fruit, had no other recourse than to flee with the boy and seek refuge with the four half-secularized nuns who watched over the church and its parish priest. They refused to accept them; the two children found shelter in the spindle trees surrounding the pedestal of the statue of the Virgin at the entrance to the village, where they spent the night. In the morning, when they finally dared to return to Puypouzin and ask to be married, the old man threatened them with his stick and chased them away despite the mother's pleas. The nuns finally took Marie on as a servant; François had passed his exams and had begun his studies to become a law clerk when the war of 1914 took him away. He returned from it a captain and one-armed, and before marrying Marie he went to ask permission. The old man took no notice of the stripes; he only saw the missing arm, and two were needed to push a plow or plant a garden. Law clerk or farmer, for him it was all the same thing. Later, when he learned that François had bought his practice, he said only, as though seized with a kind of regret, "When you know the law well, at least you know how to use it, to quietly stash away tons of money."

Lortier had bought the house about twenty years earlier from a sad and elegant woman named Marie. Supported by the saying that you don't mount a horse on a donkey, the mason had refused to rebuild the low rooms on the back gate beams eaten away by rabbit sweat. It was now a canopy of tiles sheltering a great wooden portal in which was cut the little door for rabbits. The old terraced courtyard, which had been won from the valley by flanking it with a supporting wall, was made up of hard, resonant stone, and then lawn where the arbor, cast under an old spell according to which the growing flowers awaited the bullfinches, was separated from the vegetable garden by a garden of flowers. From where he was, Lortier saw the dormer window glinting beside his library, in the tower, and the large windows that someone had succeeded in opening in the enormous walls over the valley. He knew little of the history of Puypouzin before old Baudou's generation, except that the house, it was said, had been sacked by the Huguenot troops of Agrippa d'Aubigné retreating to La Rochelle, before it was devastated by the Marcillac dragoons a hundred years later, who did their henchman apprenticeships without worrying too much about on which side, Calvinist or Catholic, the baptism had taken place. The Protestants had held out. In the village they were sometimes called the *sègre dare* in the local dialect because more than three centuries earlier, that is what they answered children who were awakened in the night to flee into the wilderness and who asked where they were going: *T'as qu'à suivre derrière.* And some families still kept the lead tokens that granted safe conduct to the assemblies. All that blood had dried, the walls were still there, stronger than history. It seemed to Lortier that houses gradually shape men, and he was an old man deeply in accord with his old house.

Swinging his small wooden tub in one hand, he followed the little path to the first stubble field wall. While waiting for the shepherds and shepherdesses to cross the bridges, he searched along its edge for big red slugs, sat down, back to the stones, removed the little bag hiding the contents of his bucket, and revealed the folded lines and the row of lead weights at the end of each one. Alongside were rolled the finer lines and their hooks. He threaded one of them into a long needle, which he pierced through the slug before securing it onto the iron hook, then knotted the line to the leaded loop of the thicker line. He didn't know what pain he inflicted there. He knew nothing of the pain of eels who might struggle all night, ripped apart by fishhooks, and no doubt he was also a henchman himself. When the lines were ready, he headed straight down, half hidden by the wall, to the place where the bend in the stream nearly met the bottom of the slope. He rediscovered the fresh and childlike pleasure of listening to flowing water and followed the alders along the shore, where wagtails were still scurrying about, to the deeper pools, where here and there, according to the current, he threw the first lines, which he then attached to the low branches. He stopped a little before Pont-Bertand: a few latecomers were still calling in the Noue to round up their cows and he wanted to be there alone, not so much because his fishing was forbidden as to avoid being seen by anyone and risking his lines being visited by an earlier riser than himself.

He sat down at the foot of an ash tree and lit a cigarette. The evening slowly darkened the meadows. He waited, concealed, without really knowing if what added to the pleasure of eating the eels was the secrecy of the poaching; or a very old taste for seizing, capturing, and abducting; or the solitary imitation of gestures never forgotten from childhood. And his grandfather was suddenly standing near him as he so often did, whistling, in the process of teaching him how to knot the line, both originator and patron of all adventure, exactly the role that time itself played for him. All his life, Lortier had humbly tried to draw knowledge from time, to extract from it its testimony by unearthing from the four corners of the world stone mallets or flint axes or bone tools and ornaments, to compare what time had left behind a few thousand years ago with what a few lost peoples had inherited from it in the forgetfulness of their old age, to decipher through it the engravings, the paintings, the marks—on rocks or in tombs—foretelling the species' first bursts of spirit. Beyond his own existence, it seemed to Lortier— forever holding his grandfather's hand—that other very ancient pasts that still welled up in him had mysteriously constructed him.

The sound of a car drew him out of his reverie, and to his amazement, coming down from a distant hamlet, perhaps the Tauderie or Aigonnay, he saw a police van crossing over the bridge to the village, followed by an ambulance. Maybe someone was sick down there or having a difficult labor, even though the police hardly had any place in all that. The cars climbed the hill, disappeared. He listened. The Noue was as empty as two or three years ago, when all the young men in his network waited with him for the plane dropping weapons. He cut straight toward the narrows of the stream between two thick piles of rocks, which might have once supported some fishing apparatus, and hung his lines in the bends where the current came to wash up against the old walls of the stream bank. He could see just enough to attach them. The sky had grown darker. In this ageless valley where he revived the ancient gestures of fishing, that police van had left a mark belonging to the evils that he would read about in his evening newspaper, an echo of his own time with its own share of savagery, struggle, deception, falsehood, and integrity, the endless confrontation of good and evil, its injustices still outraging him as in the past when he fought so hard against them. Though for all, no longer urging him into action or to take up arms. Maybe because injustice was married to an evil more terrible than itself, cruelty, against which he felt powerless. Or maybe because he had aged, as simple as that. More inclined now toward considering than combat. A little ashamed of his good luck, always asking himself what he had done to deserve it. Always hungry for the future, even if it was linked to the past by his very life, exactly in the image of this village. This evening awaiting tomorrow because Mo would be there tomorrow as she was every evening. Mo was his future.

He returned very rapidly to the bridge, walked along the wash-ing place, and took the path bordered by a wall marking the foot of the stubble fields from which the bare slope rose toward the sky's remaining light. Light seemed to rise from the meadows them-selves, covered with a light, softly glistening film the spiders had extended over the grass in weaving their webs—borne, stitch by stitch, on the breeze the day's heat made rise, as if they had leaped here and there to leave the pale traces of a stationary rain shower. Lortier rejoiced at these first gossamer threads announcing the season. The bats were hunting, and their flight made the bushes rustle as they passed, and the white moon that spanned April to singe May with its frosts appeared over the poplars. When he heard the singing of the brook he cut diagonally across to the slope, which he slowly climbed, saving his breath, until he turned onto the little road that revealed the house. A single window was lit. Without knowing why, he thought of a lantern of the dead, that hollow stone column standing in another village's cemetery, into which, in the past, a child might slip and light a lamp that shone all night to guide lost souls to the blessed earth. Standing still, he heard his fast-beating heart calm down after the climb. He loved this light, shining twenty-four meters away from him like a beacon.

He and Mo were old now, rich with grandchildren. With her usual realism, Mo considered old age calmly, like a slow and unavoidable accident, its inconveniences useless to dwell upon. Sometimes Lortier hoped he would die before she did and immediately felt ashamed at the selfishness of his wish, knowing very well that the last present he could give her would be to take on the grief of surviving. He smiled, thinking how in the past he had questioned himself about her love or about his own love for her, asking himself if they were in step, anguished or transported, living in the dazzle of this love, which supported, tortured, made up his existence. It was the blaze from a sunlit fountain, which sometimes reached a depth nearly darkening it, full of whirling leaves whose vortex he feared but that, one by one, settled gently on the bottom, without the water ever overflowing the pool or losing its crystal transparency. They were that very water, he and Mo, they were like the house; their fortress had been stronger than the years, which had worn themselves out against those walls. Perhaps they had never been so fulfilled by each other as now, when each had become for the other both the lover and child.

Lortier quickens his pace, closes the door of the little side entrance, and goes to the window of the room where Mo is seated under the lamp, her body turned toward a book propped on the table, which she is reading at the same time as she knits. When he taps on the window, her white head will rise, her face smile gently. Lortier marvels that such a source of happiness doesn't run dry.

fernand and clémence

"HERE," FERNAND HAD SAID, setting down the wheelbarrow full of beets beside her, "clean these."

Beginning from that moment when he handed his own work over to her, Clémence knew he would disappear more and more often, would be more and more vague, confused, unsteady; at supper, he would fall asleep in his chair, unless some overlooked detail provoked him into a rage, and at night, when she had the courage to go to bed, she would lie there, in the dark, beside a drunk.

In the beginning, her parents slept in the scrollwork bed draped with long curtains hanging as a canopy attached to the beams, in the back of the room where they lived. She and Fernand had the little room in the loft, her room as a child, which they preferred to the lower room behind the back kitchen, the grandfather's room. That was another life, a forgotten life. Then they themselves had slept in the big room, and the attic room had become Adrien's. Finally, despite her calm nature, she could no longer stand it that the bed was always there, a part of every hour of her life. Sometimes she needed to be alone. Zacharie, the carpenter, had moved the bed into what had once been the dining room, a room with a parquet floor that, when she was a child, was opened once or twice a year for great feasts, and that was still permeated with the odors of the closed dark, old mildew, aging wax, and tablecloths folded away long ago in the huge armoires, never to serve any purpose again.

Some nights, when Fernand returned late from the field with André, the hired hand, a kind of joy from working his land again kept him from the bottle. He looked after the animals, measured the horse's oats, put everything in order with almost too much care, then settled himself under the lamp with Adrien's notebook, helped him do his problems, and had him recite his lessons. Clémence leaned beside them at the hearth, hanging the soup pot back up on the rack or taking a shovel full of coals, which she put in the kitchen grate. She listened to Fernand add his own knowledge to what the books said, especially in arithmetic and history, about which he'd forgotten nothing. Sometimes he closed the notebook to give his own lessons, telling Adrien about green manure and leaving land fallow, about clover and alfalfa cut early—taking on the taste of toasted caramel as silage, which animals love—about how you can tell wheat is ripe when the ear tilts over and the stalk "makes a gooseneck." Those evenings, he and Clémence talked, and there was a sort of truce, even if, after the little one went to bed, he drank many glasses of wine, one after the other, very quickly, for which his body suddenly had a vital need. Those peaceful days offered no hope, however, and Clémence no longer ever thought about what Fernand had once been: strong, determined, obstinate, interested in everything, with a mind so sharp that sometimes certain neighbors, making sure his father-in-law didn't see them, came to ask him about manures or fertilizers. His knowledge of farming had a sort of prescience to it; he could divine what it was the soil needed.

In her extreme fatigue, Clémence even forgot the image of her husband that she now had, that of a heavy man, stocky, violent, with red and lifeless eyes, clumsy hands. She sat down in the barn, spread a sack over her knees, picked up a big knife, put a tub on the ground beside her, and began to peel the beets one by one. She wanted most of all to think of nothing but what she was doing, of the blade that scraped off the dry earth and sometimes revealed a tongue of pink pulp under the purple skin, of the earth that fell crumbling into the tub, of the ringing sound of the beet as she tossed it into the root slicer. When it was full, she would decide if another half a wheelbarrow load was necessary. She no longer carried the tub of earth out to the garden as in the past. She emptied it onto the pile that she had been accumulating gradually in the barn. Maybe someday she would ask André to get rid of it. André was a valiant old man who, on top of what Fernand told him to do, helped her out as much as he could. Afterward, some alfalfa had to be cut in the pasture for the rabbits; nettles along the wall had to be cut to be chopped up and mixed into the ducks' feed; bran and flour had to be measured for the pig, whom she already heard grunting. As soon as the little one returned, it would be time to milk, unless she could milk the goats later, during the night, after supper, which also had to be made. And in this vague succession of tasks, which she guessed was still incomplete, she had the clear vision of something she'd forgotten to do that made her interrupt the motions she completed mechanically, nearly in her sleep: she hadn't cleaned the milk buckets, which she still scoured with a handful of nettles until they shone.

What Clémence dreaded more than anything was the morning, the lucidity that comes from a good night's sleep: she needed a kind of dullness, a vague link between her night and what was beginning again. One day at the Pont-Bertrand washing place, Léa had said, "In the morning when it's clear, it makes it hard to see one's misery." That was exactly what she wanted to escape. She lived by night alone, perhaps vaguely putting off the moment she would lie down next to Fernand, waiting especially for the fog that hid her condition from her to thicken with the hours. She sometimes milked her goats or her cows when everyone was asleep. The night before Adrien's birthday, she had mixed her batter and made waffles toward morning. She no longer knew if sleep escaped her or if she was the one who refused it. Sometimes it triumphed, and she fell asleep in a chair, her head in her arms resting on the table. One day when she had wanted to rest, staying for once to watch her goats while she shelled peas, she had dozed off in the grass and had sunk into a bottomless pit of sleep, so sound that Adrien, in coming to find her, had said to himself: "What's that pile of rags over there? Really, that can't be my mother, can it?" All the same, she had the strength to laugh about it when he told her. She had to forget that she had once been a proud woman.

Clémence heard the sound of the herds on the road and the cries of the returning children. She got up, shook the dirt from the sack, and crossed the barnyard to open the gate. Adrien hadn't returned with the others from the Guérinière; he must have taken the other, slightly longer road, past the Bastière, to give his Maria a kiss. She wondered if she was jealous of Maria or if she was grateful for her affection for the little one. She told herself that she loved Adrien without knowing how to show him. Here was a tender, happy child, while she felt coarse and sad. But she refused to imagine she had failed at this, too. With all her strength, she refused her despair.

The storeroom adjacent to the shed had been hollowed out of the ground and its walls extended aboveground to support a loft where nuts and apples were dried on the wire mesh racks. Fernand went down the broken steps, out of habit, leaning on the iron hook embedded in the stone where there used to be a rope to keep the casks from falling. He smiled to himself at the fresh smell carried in on the slight draft from the basement window, left the door half opened onto the semidark with the four lined-up sleeping casks, the racks, the iron bottle rack where a few empty bottles were stuck upside down by the necks, and sat down on an old milking stool, entirely absorbed by the burning emptiness that the need for alcohol bored into him. Mechanically, he struck the cask with one finger, the reassuring dull thud indicating the level. He reached behind him into its home in the wall for the jam jar that had become his measure, filled it, and sadly breathed it in. He no longer knew what he suffered from, this blessed inferno that ravaged him, or this wine that appeased it. In huge swallows, he emptied the jar.

In the beginning, when he had come into this house, no one could have predicted what he really had to call his downfall. The marriage had been a superb one. Old Largeau hadn't been the poorest man in the village and Clémence had, as they say, a well-soiled petticoat. And he hadn't come into this family with only a knife in his pocket, either. His father had given him four good hectares of wheat fields on Alleray, a little vineyard at the Pérère, a little acacia woods for making posts, and the big pasture behind Puypouzin—not counting what would come to him later. Clémence was pretty, her hair parted down the middle and tightly braided, as black as her eyes. Her high forehead, white as a hawthorn blossom, counterbalanced a determined chin and large mouth always ready to laugh. She was strong, she had large, working hands, she loved to make love. He took her in the hayloft or sometimes, when she was watching the herd at Champarnaud and he was working on the Outremont, weeding his beets or sewing his barley, he left his work and rushed over to lower her into the grass, without anyone ever coming upon them as they made love. It was agreed that they would settle at the Guérinière, one of the two servants would be let go, and the two couples would run the farm, without any talk about it being divided up or who would be in control. Grandfather Largeau was still alive at that time, sitting all day in his easy chair next to the fire, suffering from a strange illness that made him laugh until he cried anytime he spoke, drowning his words in the tears of enormous laughter, sobbing with laughter when he recounted the riches of his youth—when he hitched up three mules with bells, despite the Protestant austerity of his now deceased wife, who had had a servant and wore black gloves to go to church.

In the beginning, the importance of the farm had intoxicated Fernand. He had studied the fields one by one, analyzed the land—under the mocking eye of his father-in-law—as he had learned to do in agricultural school, observed how it held water, tamed its various resistances to the plow and the way in which it crumbled under the harrow. He knew how to manage all of that, but old Clotaire had not given him more than his due. That wasn't his way, his chin was set

even more squarely than his daughter's, and he rebelled against all
novelty. He had decided once and for all upon the crop rotation for
his fields. He refused to replace his own grain with more productive
seed, accused the wind of breaking his wheat stalks when it was
because of too much nitrogen in his fertilizer, and was violently
opposed to the cemetery field—which sloped and had always been
worked end to end—being worked crosswise, even though for years
the runoff had been carrying away good soil. Even the lands that
Fernand had contributed got away from him. Little by little, they
became mixed in with the Largeaus', gradually annexed by Clotaire
and ruled by him. The same for money: Clémence got the egg and
milk money, but for days she hesitated to ask her father for it. The
young people's work added to what they would have later in this
case, too, but this "later" hardly put them at ease.

At first, Fernand went along with it all. Clémence's skin was
white and soft, he loved to work, they could look forward to the
days ahead! When it was dry and he reached the flat fields with his
horse and reaper, the light morning breeze passed gently over the
golden oats, blurred the gray of the wheat, intensified over the sup-
ple fur of the hay, rippling white. As the sun rose in the sky, the
cypress in the little cemeteries in the corner of the fields shim-
mered peacefully, the sunflowers all lifted their heads, a tawny
weasel cut in front of Fernand from left to right. This was a good
omen. A great ardor stirred in him. He felt like a king, and at the
same time it seemed to him he belonged to all this beauty. He
loved the earth with all his might, with a passion much more
ancient than himself; he loved the mystery, the signs, the things
from the past, the forgotten times, the endlessly renewed germi-

nation of old seed into new grain. His favorite field was the one called the Alaric field, where one day his plow had unearthed the large blade of a warped spear equipped with a hook, its sharp edge used perhaps to cut horses' hocks, a double hatchet, the iron inlaid with copper arabesques, and, farther on, a very ornate spur with huge teeth on the rowel and some bones. He had patiently scraped the rust off his finds and had wanted to decorate the walls of their room with them, but Clémence had rejected these treasures that resembled old useless tools. Maybe they still lay in some corner of the attic, unless Adrien had discovered them.

Fernand was weak. His dreams of the future took the place of the present for him. He realized too late that he lacked courage, that he had lands of his own in all this, that he had to take a stand, assert his views, establish boundaries and shares. Out of cowardice, and because his love for Clémence dissuaded him from it, he had given up heated discussions and refused to live in discord with his father-in-law. He had patiently accepted his troubles; Clotaire was getting old, but his hope lay especially in Adèle, his mother-in-law: a thin, unassuming woman who no longer went to church except on holidays, whose goodness had found another form of prayer. She had discovered a distant relative, very old and nearly infirm, who lived alone near the fountain of Sorigné in a large house isolated from the village, an ancient freestone structure built in the middle of the last century when farmers suddenly grew rich discovering they could double their harvests by liming old plots of land. Justine lived there with her two dogs, one of whom was let out at night, and the other, full of fleas, was tied to the foot of her bed. She was deathly afraid as soon as the night fell but gay and talkative, singing old songs, telling how her father had been wounded by the Prussians at Gravelotte and how during World War I, she had happily worked on bombs in the factory. Adèle had cleaned off, cared for, nurtured this attachment. She had suffered the dogs, scoured the house, burned the old papers. She had even cleared a corner of the old vegetable garden where zinnias, French marigolds, and gillyflowers now grew at the foot of ancient, nearly purple roses that scented the air. Every day before noon she came to help Justine get up. Every evening she brought her half a pail of soup, which the old woman divided between herself and her dogs. In the end, she spent more and more time in that house, as if little by little, the care that she lavished upon Justine had replaced the tenderness that she would have wanted to show the grandson Clémence had not given her.

Clotaire's intentions were less generous. With the permission that Adèle had to ask for and that Justine would have been hard-pressed to refuse, he put his animals in the large meadow adjoining the house and cultivated a superb field left fallow for ages, well-rested soil he only had to nourish with a year of rye grass and red clover turned under as green manure. Fernand himself thought about the house. Once the old woman died and the legal papers were put in order, he and Clémence would settle there. At first, this might be difficult, since they had no savings, but with his own lands, those that his father would certainly leave him, the Sorigné fields, and the two or three cows and meadows that his father-in-law might leave them, he would be master of his own home, cultivate it as he wished, and he and Clémence would be alone at meals, alone to talk, alone to decide things, alone to live.

But it was Adèle who had died. She had been buried at the bottom of the meadow, behind the barns, in her family's little cemetery with the three cypress trees. And with her was buried Fernand's dream. Clémence, on the other hand, had become mistress of the farmyard and the housework, in a house where she had always lived, getting more attention from her father, whom she so strongly resembled, than he had ever shown his deceased wife. She continued as her mother had done, though no doubt more coldly, to care for Justine, who had become deaf but remained cheerful. She had to treat the dogs for fleas again. She had forgotten the promises formerly associated with this house that she maintained out of duty, as she did the old woman, and she no longer ever thought she would live there: she ruled over her own.

Something of the love that Fernand bore for his wife died then. They no longer shared the same domain. His hands were tied, without even rebellion—which Clémence would not have understood —as an outlet. As a last resort, the only right that he had angrily claimed was the horses' care. There, Clotaire understood, he had to give in. No one other than Fernand hitched up the horses, fed them, or groomed them. As for the rest, he continued to sow the old seed, to rotate the same crops in the same fields, to ignore the new fertilizers, to work the cemetery fields lengthwise, to take orders. He had become his father-in-law's servant, and Clémence's servant, too. He drank. Wine clouded over the day with a light haze that masked the time, hid the immutable future, warmed the sort of cold his alienation produced in him.

Years later, Clotaire ended up taking old Largeau's place in the corner by the fire, oblivious to all, recognizing no relatives or neighbors except his daughter, who made him eat. They put him, as his precursor before him, into the little room behind the back kitchen. He hardly ever left his bed then and finally kicked the bucket. Fernand became the master, but it was too late. At that point, the war began and disrupted everything. He was sent close to the Belgian border; it was almost his first trip. He spent months waiting, then fighting in incredible confusion and retreating farther and farther with fewer and fewer men. They were no more than a handful at Libourne, where they were demobilized and sent back home. From this incomprehensible torture, he had retained the feeling of belonging, despite himself, to a world that was absolutely foreign to him. Uneasiness and sorrow had also drawn him closer to the bottle then.

Upon his return, Justine was no longer there. The spring following his mobilization, Clémence had been very sick. She had been delirious, and Madame Lortier had taken care of her. André, the hired hand, ran from the fields to the stables, the stables to the house. His wife had come to take care of the farmyard animals, and everyone had forgotten Justine. When Clémence was able to remember her, André had rushed over to Sorigné. The yellow dog was howling in the courtyard, the old woman was stone dead, and the other dog chained to the bed had begun to eat her. The smell of death had driven him mad and he had to be shot.

Too late. Going over and over his life was useless. Fernand refilled his jar from the tap, breathed in the wine, and gazed for a long time at its purple sheen. The cellar had become his refuge, his hiding place haunted with dreams buried there. Too late. The Sorigné house had been rented, half the land had been rented, and what remained was enough. With André, they got by. And it was easy to see that his only joy now was Adrien, even though he was often hard on him when he was drunk, when the whole world was hard. He still regretted the day he'd struck him so brutally, beaten him because of that swollen cow the boy had left to wander in the alfalfa. All he wanted to dream about was the happiness of the fishing expeditions that brought them close. Sometimes the thought of Adrien erased the wine, and he temporarily regained his strength, harnessed the horse to the cart, and went into the fields with André, rediscovering the effort and the pleasure of former times, a kind of hope. He loved to help Adrien with his homework, discovering his former learning to be intact and passing it on to him. Those days he told himself that when Adrien grew up, he would take him along into the fields, into the woods, would gradually teach him his own knowledge of the land and all it required. He didn't dare kiss Adrien. He no longer kissed anyone. Clémence rejected his touch. One day Valérie Faucheux, who was so proud of her eighteen years, had come to pester him in his cellar. She offered him her breasts, the little slut; he staggered as he tried to grab her, and she jumped to one side. She duped him: his hand could never reach her, and she had run away, laughing at him. He had fallen back onto his stool and begun to cry. He also had to talk to Adrien about girls, later. When Adrien got married, he would break the lease on his grandfather's old house, the one he loved so much, which was rented. He would pay the penalty and go live there with Clémence, if she wanted to. Never would Adrien and his wife live with him and Clémence, never! Adrien would have the Guérinière all to himself. He drank deeply. The emptiness within him still burned. He filled the jar again.

"So what were you doing?" cried Clémence when the boy had closed the gate behind the animals. "Was it your Maria who made you dawdle at the Bastière again? Have they had water?"

"Yes, at Pont-Bertrand."

"Then put them in, the bedding's all done. Afterward, let the horse out."

Adrien pretended to hurry the cows along, though they were finding the way to the stable all by themselves. He hitched them one by one with a motion he enjoyed very much because he had to put both his arms around their necks and press his cheek against their rough reddish hair to attach the chain. The little goat had already rushed to his mother's teat. Adrien petted him for a long time, then slipped into the stable to undo the horse, who occupied only one of the four stalls; the others now stored tools or the hay in which his father sometimes slept. He was always a little afraid of going in there. The horse needed only to lean its enormous weight against the partition to crush him. He undid the tether and went ahead of him, listening to the sound of hooves ringing on the stable tiles, then muffled in the yard, a loud sound, safe, which gradually erased the terror mixed with a secret glory that he still felt from his discovery. He had needed to see Maria. She had heard the herd, the only one to take that route when Adrien went the long way. She had come to the gate with a big smile of pleasure, they'd exchanged a few words, she thought he looked pale, but perhaps it was the time of day that gave him that gray hue. She had run to the house and brought back a sweet crêpe. Hearing her calm voice, returning to the safety of the village, the oppression that stifled Adrien lifted. The animals had continued on without waiting for him, and he had set off to catch up with them, still agitated but no longer over-whelmed as the turmoil subsided. The horse sniffed at the water a long time, snorting with pleasure, and now was drinking. With each big mouthful, his nostrils gently rose and fell. Adrien stared at the bottom of the large stone trough where a few crayfish from the stream were hidden under the tiles. A dead man had once lain in this sarcophagus. The horse was drinking from a tomb. He told himself that he now possessed a great secret that set him apart even more, even if he was still the little boy he looked like in the eyes of everyone else.

Suddenly Fernand appeared from nowhere, red-faced and drunk, his eyes bloodshot. The blow was over like that, so power-ful the child staggered.

Fernand stammered furiously, "I'm the one who takes care of the horse. No one but me, ever, you understand? Ever!"

Adrien held his cheek, without a tear. Fernand tore the lead rope from his hand, violently pulling on the horse, who still want-ed to drink, and marched stiffly toward the stable, very straight, as if he were concentrating on not wavering from his line. Soon he came out, passed the barn where Clémence stood wordlessly watching him, and went into the shed where he could be heard banging the iron tools, as if he were letting out his anger on them. Adrien slowly moved away from the racket. Something hard and cold as ice weighed in his chest. Clémence came toward him and held him against her, kissing him, gently caressing his cheek. She remembered too late that in the past, the horse had been Fernand's exclusive domain.

"My little rabbit," she said softly, "don't be afraid. He isn't wicked. It's my fault. It's because of me. He's always gone crazy over that horse, it's his property."

She cried, two big tears that glistened as they fell, heavy and slow. Adrien looked at her, cried, "Maman! Maman!" and nestled against her blouse. Then they drew apart and Adrien went to talk to the little goat.

At supper, Fernand had calmed down and was nearly cheerful, sometimes chuckling low in his throat, as if he were laughing at himself. He questioned Adrien on his lessons, but this was just routine. He had that unsteady, far-off voice that the child knew so well. Getting up, he placed his hand on the boy's head and ruffled his hair, looking at him solemnly, and then, without saying a word, disappeared. Clémence was tired. She forced herself to smile while Adrien prepared his schoolbag, drew him close to her, and held him a long time, her lips pressed to the boy's forehead. When Adrien was in bed, she climbed the steps heavily to tuck him in and kissed him again. This wasn't customary. He felt proud and happy. What earned him these tendernesses was now subdued, sleeping in a secret memory.

When Clémence went back down to the kitchen, the table wasn't cleared. She reminded herself that she still hadn't milked the goats, looked at the clock, and sat down. It suddenly seemed to her that this was the end of her life; she could no longer face it. She could no longer keep everything clean and put away, she could no longer keep up with everything, complete it. There was laundry to do in the back kitchen, dirt under the table. The dirt was winning. However much you swept every day, the dirt had to be driven back outdoors. The bedroom was dirty. She should make the bed, sweep again, stop because the time to milk the goats had come and gone. It was too late. There were also the dishes to do. Once more, she imagined that maybe she could get a servant, but she didn't have the time to look for one. She was too tired. She lit the hurricane lamp, turned off the light, watched the red glow of the fire for a long time, tried to not think anymore. Her only wish was to be sitting there, in front of the coals, in the dark, her hands on her knees, waiting.

V

zacharie

"**NINE TIMES OUT OF TEN**, it's for money," said Zacharie Métivier, called Va-Devant, putting his plane down on the workbench. "I can tell you what happened to my grandfather's father."

"Yes, but this time, it can't be for money," said Lortier. "I can't get over this story."

"That's why nobody can understand it. Now, my grandfather's father, that's not today, of course, but at least it was clear. My father said that he was a very able man, you know what he was? During his seven years of service, he had become a master of foot boxing, using leg-work or a cane, yes, my friend!"

Seated on the stool, Lortier listened patiently to his old friend, breathing in that fresh scent of wood he had associated with the memory of this well-ordered workshop ever since his childhood, the iron tools with their worn and shining handles, the piles of shavings and sawdust swept over by the door where a few cobwebs, thick with the dust from sanding, hung as drapery. He and Zacharie went back to school days, his father chatted with Moïse Métivier, Zacharie's father, while he rolled a cigarette, just as he himself was doing now. No time had passed, hardly a life. It was a moment full of echoes, darkened by what he had just learned.

"So the old man sets off for La Mothe to sell two steer," said Zacharie, fitting a screwdriver in his bit brace. "He does business with two guys who call themselves butchers in Pamproux, they drink a bottle of wine, and these two guys pay for the steer all in small coins, two heavy sacks of them. The old man heads home on foot, and when he reaches the Hermitain forest, he cuts himself a big chestnut stick, because from the first he says to himself that if he's been paid with these two sacks, it's to keep his hands tied up: if he's attacked, he'll have to drop them to defend himself. And since the road goes straight through the middle of the forest, when night comes, he watches behind him and sees shadows following him without making any sound, walking on the grass along the side. He turns suddenly into the forest, hides his sacks, and waits. The shadows arrive and he hears them talking in very low voices: 'I'm sure that I saw him there. Where could he have gone? Where is he?' Then the old man shouts out loud, 'Here I am!' and leaps onto the road. Before you know it, the stick comes down on the first one's forehead, who falls flat and doesn't move; the other one comes up, his knife out, the stick knocks him in the legs with one end, the kidneys with the other, there he is crawling along. The old man frisks them, takes their knives, goes to find his two sacks, and continues peacefully on his way. All that to say they might easily have had their throats slit, those two crooks, and why? To get two steer without paying for them. Crimes like that, it's always for love or money, everyone knows that. Money spoils everything, by God!"

"And were you always as tough as the old man with your journeyman's stick?" asked Lortier, smiling.

"Well, when I was young, I wasn't so easy to catch," said Zacharie, who had slipped his screws into the holes and tightened them. "But four years in the trenches first, and then, twenty years later, this mess we just got ourselves out of, well, the taste for battle's left me, you can understand."

The First World War had taken Zacharie off after his apprenticeship tour. He had had more luck than Lortier. He had gotten through the whole thing without being wounded, and that luck had continued to protect him during the war that had just ended. He no longer believed in much of anything. He no longer had faith in anything but his hands, the frank and quiet strength of the wood, the strict brotherhood and code of the guild, which brought together all that he had been taught as a child. A few years before the war he had been affiliated as an aspiring *menuisier du Devoir,* and his admission work was still in a room that he almost never opened: an arched carriage entrance on two levels, with two doors, two huge frames, the posts, crosspieces, casings in walnut, the panels and motifs in very finely jigsawed and molded linden, with a purity of proportion that almost seemed a reflection of the upright and generous nature his sponsors had to have sensed in calling him Poitevin Noble Coeur. He had shown Lortier the notebook from his tour, full of drawings of what he had seen or done, of steps with complicated gyrons, shafts with sculpted scrolls, arched panels of church pulpits or cupolas for which he had taken down cross-section plans and measurements.

Zacharie talked endlessly of work, as he had all his life. Lortier looked for signs of aging in his old companion, the aging he recognized and accepted calmly enough in himself, a bald head crowned with a ring of white curls that made him look like Saint Joseph in the paintings, the heavy eyes with the sometimes absent gaze of a man returning from far off, two deep lines that made his cheeks fall and gave his mouth an almost bitter expression, all that contradict-ed nevertheless by a quick and jovial nature, forever tempted by the pleasure of storytelling. The workshop had spared him the mark of farmers, that forehead divided by a neat line separating wind and sunburn from white skin, perpetually protected by a cap or beret, but the mark of his trade was on his left middle finger, which only had two phalanges left, the third having slipped under an electric planer's blade into the hole left by a splintered pine knot.

"Without telling you what to do," said Zacharie, "you are going to help me. Oak boards like that, they don't give like willow. You see, they always say you end up between four boards, but no, you end up between six! This doesn't happen to me often, making two caskets at once."

"Who was it that found them?"

"You won't believe it: Lebraut."

"Lebraut? What was he doing there?"

"He was hunting for morels, the lazybones. He was useful, for once!"

Lebraut did not rank high in the village hierarchy, as much based on belonging to landowning families and respecting the customs as on wealth. The true village ended with the hired hands who had nothing and were often drinkers, rough as barley bread. Once the wine was paid for, these families lived as they could on the rest of a peasant's salary. But the community—seemingly unified even if, in

watching out for itself, it spied on, envied, or secretly betrayed itself
—considered them its own. On the other hand, it brutally rejected
the stragglers passing through, the tinkers, the gypsy vendors selling
colored baskets and lace. Between hired hands and Bohemians, it
tolerated but kept at its edges a few rebels who had established
themselves there, responding to distant kinships with the country
where they spoke the local dialect. They were badly paid when
needed for work and had no connection to the community other
than as merchants and to scare and entertain the children. Lebraut
belonged to this fringe element.

"You should have seen him putting on airs," said Zacharie,
pressing down on his clamp. "Straight, lean, sunken cheeks, still in
that white shirt he wears to go through the village and buy his bread
without greeting anyone, his tight jacket, his canvas pants, and his
espadrilles, summer or winter. Not to mention his straw hat. This
time he wasn't selling escargots or mushrooms, he wasn't collecting lichen from the pines or wild narcissus for the perfume makers.
No, this was Monsieur Lebraut, proprietor, who was leading the
police for once. And it's true, that roof he lives under, the half that
hasn't collapsed yet, does belong to him, from his mother."

Lebraut lived by gathering, only accepting work when
absolutely necessary, only approaching society stealthily, with the
exception of its prisons, which he sought out in the depths of winter when he got too cold. And to which he gained access thanks to
a good meal he couldn't pay for in a restaurant in Niort. Zacharie
said that he had gone to get warm at Widow Woe's Place. A few
military eccentricities, like the obscenity tattooed on his right palm
to get himself exempted from saluting, had gotten him sent to the

disciplinary battalions in Africa, and that was about all anyone knew of his past. Except that Marie-sans-Couette, his mother, an old washerwoman skinning her hands for bread and board, had given birth to him one July 14 in the guardroom, a sort of cell that was always open, strewn with straw, and waiting to lock up whatever poacher the rural police caught. This miserable birth, which had nevertheless earned him the nickname of République, might have been one of the obscure reasons for an anarchism condemned to secrecy by his poverty.

"So here's our Lebraut going to the mayor, the mayor calling the police, and Lebraut telling his story, taking his time. He was on the Outremont, not on his side, on the plateau above the Charconnier stubble fields. He was visiting his morel spots, there's some broom above those fields, it's pretty poor. He passes the hedge, he stays close to the cultivated fields, and all of a sudden what does he see on the cart path along the hedge? A man lying on his stomach on the ground, at the corner of a square of half-sown corn, face in the dirt, next to an opened bag of seed. Lebraut, he's suspicious, and he wonders what kind of trick's being played on him, just his luck. He calls out, 'Yo! Yoo-hoo! Everything okay?' The man doesn't budge. Even so, he wants to be sure about this character with his nose pushed into the dirt. He pokes him a little with his stick, still he doesn't budge. He leans over to grab him by the shoulder and shake him and then, I tell you, he sees the back shot through and covered with blood, the man already stiff, and when he turns him over, the chest is pulp, and he recognizes Clairon, Fréchaud by his real name, a good hired hand who lives with his wife in the Raymondière, near you. Dead. Stiff as a board. With eyes wide open, and the mouth of someone who could have been crying for help. He's scared, Lebraut, he's really afraid in the open field with this corpse. For a moment, he wonders if he should run or stay put when suddenly, five or six meters away from him, he sees something else that makes his blood run cold: another body stretched out there on its back along the hedge, with one shoulder and half the neck blown off, draining into a brown pool, and he recognizes Simon Varadier, I tell you! Simon, who was old enough to be my son, a good neighbor, a boy I really liked, solid as gold, honest, always ready to help out, and now, this!"

Zacharie turned away, looking for some screws, which he didn't pick up, blew his nose noisily, grabbed a board, which he put on the end of the casket, and traced the diagonal cuts without speaking.

"I can't get over this story," Lortier repeated. "It doesn't make any sense. Fréchaud I didn't know, but Simon, I can still see him there. Didn't he have a little girl?"

Zacharie nodded his head, suddenly too upset to talk.

"Alice," he said finally.

"Right! A little pointed face with big violet eyes, I know her, that little one. My wife does drawing with her Wednesday evening, with two or three other little girls. Poor kid!"

"She's my little friend. She often comes to see me with Adrien. They get bark from the pine boards from me to make boats. And her mother, too, is as pretty as a peach. I tell you, when I measured him to make that," he said, tapping the boards with his hand, "when I saw that poor woman, so young, with the eyes of a frantic sparrow hawk! And Simon who was so bright, you would have sent him to find the dead, so sure you'd be that he'd save them, well, just thinking about him…"

Zacharie blew his nose again, made a face to check his bit brace, and lifted his steel-rimmed glasses, which were all misted over.

"Still, this beats all!" he said. "Two at one time! And not in the war, in the village! And for nothing, apparently!"

In order to wipe his eyes, he pretended to scratch his ear, from which gleamed the guild's little gold earring, which he called his joint.

"Not for the one who killed them. Surely he had a bad reason, but a reason. They still have to find who could have done it."

"Well, I might have an idea, but I wouldn't say, I'd be too afraid of being wrong. As for me, it's the reason that stumps me, two strong young guys, in perfect health, who go out to plant corn, who never did anybody any harm, and Lebraut finds them murdered."

"Two gunshots and it's not hunting season, that's clear at least."

"No. Jeandet was pounding stakes to reinforce his bank above the Noue. The kids who watch the herds said that his sledgehammer rang all afternoon like gunshots. Even Adrien, my little friend from Fernand's place, you know him, a darned alert boy, it was closest to him, and he didn't hear anything except Jeandet's sledgehammer."

"Alert, but a dreamer," said Lortier. "I know him, our Adrien, he could have imagined thirty-six battles, heard the gunshots, and believed that he was the one firing the cannon."

"And no empty cartridges at the scene, evidently. The doctor said it was number-five shot, the kind used for hares here."

"I passed the police just now coming here."

"It doesn't seem like it, but the village is completely disrupted. They're beginning to question people," said Zacharie, who was loosening the clamps. "I heard they want to see all the guns that have come out again since the war; they'll be paying you a visit. Fréchaud was a good, brave fellow, a hard worker. He had his own small field and some goats. His wife is well known for her cheeses. But they didn't have any children. They come from Gâtine. They're devout Catholics. Catholic or Protestant, as in my family or in Simon Varadier's, it's still the same good God. In my opinion, he must have been looking somewhere else, not over the Outremont yesterday."

What he had experienced and, maybe even more, the photographs revealing the unimaginable hell of the camps had estranged Zacharie from religion. Beneath his gay and mischievous appearance, he was a reticent man who spoke little of himself, just as he remained silent on the reasons for his solitude, explained by old village gossip by the tragic death, in her youth, of the woman he had loved. He preferred to tell stories of the past in which he played no role, in which the warmth of his tone erased all traces of grief, trials, hard work. In this village, which kept such a close eye on itself with its spies and its busybodies, nobody had ever suspected that for four years Zacharie had hidden English aviators in the loft above his workshop where he dried his wood, pilots in transit being transported by Lortier's network to Spain, or radio operators whose messages directed the arms drops. An ingenious system, a cord suspended in front of him, which he needed only to tug on when he saw someone entering the yard and the trapdoor of the loft would bang shut, the noise a signal for silence or, if necessary, for fleeing over the rooftops. The problem was not attracting attention for purchases requiring many more tickets than he had on his ration card. But most of the time, Lortier and his men provided bread and supplies rather than tickets. Zacharie made do by emptying his cellar. At night, the English went out to stretch their legs in the garden. He had even taken one of his boarders along to hang eel lines. The pilot rolled in the grass with pleasure.

Once, however, he had been afraid. He was so caught up in his work that he hadn't seen Gefreiter coming with four men. He hadn't had time to pull the cord. A few laughs and footsteps above had not frozen quickly enough for the corporal not to hear them. He was coming only to repost a warning that poorly concealed lights had been noticed several times in the workshop; and it was true, they went out only when orders in German were shouted from the road; the fold meant that the next time, they would shoot. Zacharie, fear in his belly, read the reprimand contritely. Then the German pointed to the gold joint in the carpenter's ear and made a questioning sign, to which Zacharie responded with another sign. His whole face lighting up with a smile, the corporal drew from his pocket a little case holding a tie pin decorated with a compass, T-square, and plane, and he whispered in a low voice, *"Vorher war ich Genosse. Vor drei und dreißig, moi Rolandsbruder, Schreimer, menuisier comme vous."* "I knew them, the Roland brotherhood," said Zacharie as he told it later, "they wear the honorable blue, the blue tie, if you prefer. They descend from the French Huguenots who fled to Germany. If I had had my stick and colors, I would have performed the welcome ceremony for him!" He had to make do with giving the extended hand a firm handshake. Then with a doubtful smile, the corporal had pointed to the loft stairs, Zacharie had slowly shook his head no, and the other one had picked up the plane on the workbench, looked at it, then carefully put it down and said, *"Bonne chance, Kamrad,"* and they had all left.

"And you, where did you hide your gun, during those four years?" asked Zacharie.

"In a beehive."

Lortier looked around the too-large workshop, the two workbenches stored away in the far end against a wall, which he had seen disorderly with work in the busy hands of two companions, not counting the apprentice. Zacharie noticed his gaze.

"Ah yes!" he said.

"You aren't going to take anyone on, for afterward?"

"Afterward? There won't be any afterward! They'll all go to Niort in their cars; we've already got five or six of them in the village. I've even heard that they're going to have motorized tractors to take the place of horses. We don't have any idea what's ahead."

"Everything changes but death."

"But all the same, until the end of time it'll be like my father read in his Bible, 'The morning comes, and also the night.' As for me, I'm nothing anymore but an old artisan infidel, by God! It was a long time ago that my father had me put my first tenon into my first mortise and said to me, 'You go to bed with the plane for one night, and you think you'll wake up a carpenter; you have a long way to go, my boy.' It's true, the way has been long. And to end up here, making two caskets at once."

"You know what I say, Zacharie? God knows we've hoped for this peace! Well, as for me, I can't get used to it. I didn't imagine it this way. And I didn't imagine myself this way."

"And that one!" said Zacharie, pointing to one of the caskets.

"Simon, four and a half years as a captive, and he comes back to get himself shot by a hunting rifle. That little woman waited years for her husband, he comes back, and now she's mourning him!"

"'Father, if I must drink this cup, let your will be done,' that's also in your Bible. To accept, that's really the most difficult thing. Nearly impossible. When are they going to be buried?"

"When the police doctor has finished his work. Me, I'll be ready tomorrow afternoon. I only need to do the moldings on that one," said Zacharie, tapping one of the lids on the workbench with his fist. "Good heartwood, when I think that poor Fréchaud's wife wanted the least expensive, pine! Of course I know that all wood's the same for the dust of the dead, but no, for the same price I've used good oak for them both; they'll pay me when they can, what else could I do? This world's wickedness, when will it come to an end?"

alice

ALICE HAD BEEN TERRORIZED by the pallor of her father's corpse. At her age, death had no meaning, and she witnessed with curiosity, without any sense of what she saw, the bleeding of rabbits and fowl or the slaughtering of pigs. She wasn't surprised when old people disappeared, everything continued as before, nothing ever ended. In that room that Léa and her aunt didn't dare forbid her to enter, she had seen only her father's face; a sheet pulled up to his chin hid the mutilated body. In that second, with a horrible fear, she had taken in death as a truth. She had not touched her father's familiar and instantly strange cheek, she had embraced death. For many days she lived with this discovery that she hadn't managed to tame. What had made such a violent rupture in her existence could not be reconciled with the whispering and silence in the house, or the murmurs and sad, merely sad, faces of the visitors. When they were alone, Léa cried with little moans of grief and anger; she hated and endured death. Those sobs were no help to the little girl; she felt wrenched by an unknown force, and she would have liked to be able to cry wildly. When Zacharie had come to measure the body, even though he had very discreetly unfolded his measuring stick and had extended it so quickly along the side of the sheet that she had hardly caught his gesture, she had understood instinctively that the corpse, which was nothing more than the form of her father now but which was there, had become the object of an inexorable process of disappearance. Leaving her mother to cry and pray, she followed Zacharie into the yard, threw her lowered head against his legs, and let out her first sobs, clinging to her old friend with all her might.

Her aunt had decided that the little one shouldn't go to the funeral. Cécile Brunet, the hairdresser, suggested she come spend the morning and have lunch with them. Madeleine Lortier had also invited her, since she and her husband had already come to offer their condolences. Léa would have liked for her to go to Puypouzin, but the aunt was strict about etiquette and since Cécile had spoken first, it was to Cécile and Germain Brunet's house that the little one would go. They would have a funeral lunch with the relatives.

The memorial service was performed in the Protestant church, without the casket. According to the country's custom followed by both religions, the mirrors had been veiled and the clock stopped. Following behind the pastor, the four pallbearers Léa had chosen, neighbors and relatives, came for Simon Varadier's body. They crossed the yard, leaning to one side to compensate for the weight of the casket, and placed it on the hearse, harnessed and waiting. Then each of them had taken hold of one of the coffin handles. The whole village followed Simon to his family cemetery, in his Alleray field. Usually the procession was a time for quiet conversations in this place where everyday life included losses, which the villagers accepted naturally, as they accepted storms, frosts, old age. This time, everyone was silent and somber in the face of an inexplicable double death that was the result of neither chance nor weather and that they didn't dare to call murder. And the old people murmured in low voices that after this burial, there would have to be another one and that no one could remember having ever witnessed such a thing. Then the hearse and horse left the road and followed a long dirt path where grass grew up between the ruts made by cart wheels. Spring was exploding, the sweet-smelling whiteness of the hawthorn hedges hummed with bees, those who walked along the side stepped on the wide leaves of the large pigweed or ducked to avoid the apple-scented wild rose branches—in such a way that this village procession, dressed in dark colors spread out in the middle of the exploding yellow of the rapeseed, seemed like a parade dedicated to the gods of the fields. Before the open grave, the pastor read the psalm "From the depths of the abyss," and then, without the sudden and noisy relief that usually follows the sadness of burials, everyone returned in funeral procession to the Catholic church where Fréchaud's body awaited them, attended by his widow and the parish priest, which they would take to the cypress grove in the Catholic cemetery after the mass. When they dispersed, the ceremonies hadn't dispelled the village's nervous unease, the burials neatly concluding death as was usually the case. Everything did not continue exactly as before. The mystery of who had done it, and why, remained.

The aunt and uncle settled into the guest room. The uncle had begun by planting leeks in the garden, then had harnessed the horse to the plow and, reclaiming his old skills, started to work the little vineyard. The aunt took advantage of Léa's collapse to take things into her own hands and buzzed around like a bee. She considered three days the proper mourning period for Alice not to be sent to school. The little girl wandered about the house and yard, surprised and quite satisfied with this special dispensation that singled her out, but she soon became bored. She who loved reading so much had forbidden herself to read, considering that during this time of mortification she ought to deny herself this pleasure. Her father's absence, which altered everything, affected her through violent and confused crises, and it was often some small thing that set them off, a half-smoked cigarette resting on the millstone, a cap she had found and hidden with her treasures. Sometimes, she was afraid. She wondered if the one who had shot her father was going to jump out from a dark corner of the barn and point his gun at her, like Javart probably aimed his at Jean Valjean, like the King of the Mountains did, and in her pocket, she clutched a certain knot she'd make in her handkerchief with all her might. Then suddenly she was calm again, absorbed in the present, lost in the solemn cheerfulness that was her mark in games at recess, and dreamily jumping rope all alone. On the second day, she was quite surprised to find that she missed homework and lessons. She watched for Albert Mainson to pass as he took his cows down to the meadows, his schoolbag on his back. Albert gave her the news: according to Rosa Mousset and Elodie Gaillot, they had been talking about her in school. The schoolmaster had forbidden them from playing murder anymore in the boys' yard and the schoolmistress had asked all the girls to act as if nothing had happened when she came back. Coming from the one who, after her father, was for her the law, this attention touched her deeply at first, and then flattered her, and she hurried

off to the lessons and arithmetic exercises Albert had brought, as if
to show her teacher how grateful she was.

She entered the courtyard in the morning at the head of an escort
of unusually quiet girls carrying themselves in a way that conveyed
sympathy. Her misfortune had made her a queen. She wavered
between making a show of abandoning herself to the grief to which
she owed this new power and priding herself on remaining tough
and strong. During the first morning recess, her sympathetic court
resumed, but soon the littlest ones began to play and conversations
started up among the older ones, who gradually drifted away for a
game of the Tower, careful of where Rosa led Alice. At that
moment, she understood that when grief overcame her, she had to
flee from the group and bear it alone.

In the boys' yard, the little girl's return revived earlier discussions on the murderer's identity. Instinctively, everyone located
him outside the village or at its fringes, some of them maintaining
that Lebraut had to be guilty even though he wasn't known to have
a gun, others talking about a mysterious gypsy who was supposedly
seen on the Outremont—they even wondered if he hadn't tried to
poison the Fontmaillol spring. Still others had supernatural explanations, growing out of stories their grandmothers told and suddenly
taking shape: the evil spells of the Ganipote, the Galery hunt, the
werewolf, or Mother Lusine. Those who lived in the hamlets and
returned from school along the thickets or on lonely paths silently
swallowed hard, thinking of the evening walk home. Adrien listened
to these conversations without taking part in them, following all

the gestures and facial expressions with the wide eyes of a reticent child.

"In any case, no one knows anything," said Albert Mainson wisely.

"All the same, you can have your suspicions."

"We'll know soon enough when he's caught," said little Henri Forestier, as quick and cunning as a weasel. "What about having some fun?"

"This is fun, isn't it," said Jeannot Lacourlie, enormously fat, stuffed into his black smock. He turned to Adrien. "What do you think about it, how come you never say anything?"

"It doesn't bring Alice's father back to her," said Adrien.

"Alice Varadier, she's going to be even more stuck up, now that everyone is looking at her."

"Leave Alice alone," said Albert Mainson.

"You aren't stuck up when something horrible's happened to you," said Adrien icily.

"It's true that she's nearly a welfare case, like you, your girl-friend, she doesn't have a father anymore."

"I have a father," said Adrien.

"A dud," said Jeannot Lacourlie, "a wine sack."

He hadn't finished his sentence before Adrien's head hit him full force right in the stomach and knocked him over. The fat boy defended himself badly. Raging, Adrien pounded savagely into that flabby flesh, its weight flattening him nevertheless, but he didn't give up: he clawed, he struck, he would have liked to strangle him, to kill him. The older Edmond broke through the circle surrounding the fighters, grabbed them calmly by the collars, and separated them, Adrien still kicking wildly. The schoolmaster had seen the crowd gather and come over.

"Hey! Hey! What's going on here?"

"It's Jublin who wanted to fight," sniveled Lacourlie.

"I don't like whining," said the teacher. "Go on, it's time, get in line. Adrien, brush off your smock, it's all dusty."

At noon, all the children from the village rushed out of the school yard into the road, shouting, singing, calling, brothers and sisters looking for each other, the older ones taking the younger ones' hands, while the children from the hamlets gathered together under the girls' covered playground and took out their packed lunches. For a moment, a guard re-formed around Alice, a wall of compassion protecting her from the boys, and then the groups disintegrated, dispersed, and re-formed according to neighborhoods. Without the others noticing him, Adrien joined those from the Bastière and walked next to Alice, in silence at first, then becoming bold enough to tell her, nearly in a whisper, that he hadn't dared to come see her.

"I know," said Alice. "You did the right thing."

"I thought it was an awful thing to happen to you."

"Really awful."

He suddenly found the word he was looking for.

"It was tragic."

"Yes, tragic. I have to talk to you in secret," said Alice. "Are you going to take your cows out to the field tomorrow?"

"Yes, of course."

"Then I'll go, if my aunt wants me to. I don't like my aunt."

"Say, Adrien," called Morisson, "what are you doing there? Have you lost your way?"

"He's allowed to," said Rosa Mousset.

"Keep us company, Adrien," cried Albert Mainson, who was gathering up burdock balls to throw onto the smocks, where they stuck. "Will you come with us this evening if we have relay races?"

Adrien had already run off.

"I'll be there," he cried, "you'll see! We'll be great! We'll be unbeatable!"

It was a beautiful day. Biting into a thick slice of buttered bread, Adrien, his bookbag on his back, ran to get in front of his herd and make them leave the straight road for a wide path marked by the dry clog prints, cutting across the thickets and following the valley under the small ash leaves, so light green that they sometimes seemed yellow, as in autumn. Adrien stood for a moment where the path opened into bare undergrowth to look at the ground, brightly colored with wood anemones. He liked to collect flowers for the pleasure of collecting them, of holding them. For one brief moment, it seemed to him that he possessed these fragile radiant delights forever. Anxious to get to the thick grass, the herd hurried across when the ford of the stream appeared in the full sunlight. Under the last trees, beside the dog violets, which had no odor, the anemones blazed. Adrien hardly had time to make a quick bouquet of them. He ran behind the cows, who were gaining their footing on the other bank, and leaped across on the flat rocks, which had been put there to avoid having to go the long way around by the bridge. The bright sunlight, the sparkling brook, the barking dogs, the cries of Albert and Rosa, who were waving wildly in greeting, all made up so joyous a welcome that suddenly the Noue was the place he loved most in the world.

One big communal meadow, very flat and flooded by winter's runoff, took up the whole valley floor between the curving alders bordering the banks and the battered slopes of little rocks on the other side. Closed off on one side by the dark barrier of a very thick hedge, it disappeared on the other side into the ethereal poplar groves where distant wood pigeons cooed. This whole place belonged to the shepherd children. It was a timeless, ageless domain where ordinary constraints were abolished in the exhilaration of freedom. Adrien ran toward the others, who had settled into one of the bends where the stream escaped to cross through the reeds, and he threw himself down near them, laughing, happy, free of everything, extending toward Rosa, the little bouquet of anemones, which she took ceremoniously and tied with a blade of grass. Almost immediately all three of them were on their feet again, calling loudly to welcome Edmond and little Alice, who arrived one after the other. Edmond waved a stick cut in the thickets, all twisted by spiraling viburnum. He hurried his cows, who set sparkling diamonds leaping from the stream as they crossed it. Behind him, Alice hopped gracefully across the stones of the ford. She seemed frail; she concentrated hard, trying not to stumble, and Adrien felt that a great silent energy lifted him toward her. At first, she appeared solemn, as she often did, but soon the children's company freed her. The vise grip of the tragedy that had so affected her relaxed its hold. Once more she was without a past, given over to the moment in which she lived, and she began to laugh and run around until she threw herself down next to Adrien, out of breath, her little heart-shaped face pink and smooth, her eyes like gold-dusted columbine still wide with rediscovered pleasure.

"What shall we do?" asked Albert.

"We'll do our lessons," said Edmond, "then we'll be done with them."

Adrien and Albert drew closer, the girls withdrew, Edmond took his books and stretched out on his stomach under an alder, which they all called *vergne*. The exuberance of arrival gave way to a studious murmur. Sometimes one of them got up to check the herds, but the cows were too busy with that succulent grass to wander into the poplars or try to break through the hedge. Albert was the first to toss his book in the air and catch it, crying, "I'm all done!" He announced that he was going to make a mill, borrowed Adrien's knife, and began to look for little forks in the branches to use. One by one, books went back into packs. Irresistibly drawn by the stream, Edmond went back toward the ruined stone pilings where broken pieces of flagstone that could have once been part of an ancient bridge made perfect retreats for crayfish at the far end. Rosa followed him. She was fascinated by the way the boy spotted something gleaming behind a rock, the big head and trembling barbels of a loach. He sometimes managed to catch one of them in a little jar, which he slid slowly behind the fish and then shot forward so suddenly the loach remained captured there. The game was often to rip it open to see the gills fluttering. Or sometimes Edmond found a molting crayfish and, with delicious horror, Rosa rolled the shell-less flesh between her fingers. The real pleasure was walking barefoot in the water.

Adrien and Alice remained alone near the reeds where the gray
and yellow wagtails at work on their nests sometimes burst out in
short flights. Engulfed in the damp odor of mint, they lay watching
for an agitation in the long leaves, invisible marsh warblers secretly
passing. Or they watched the vibrant trembling of the dragonflies,
so rapid that you couldn't distinguish the color of their wings, so
that you could make bets if they would be blue or brown when they
came to rest. Then you could pick them up, pinching together those
fragile veined almond wings and touch the long ringed body, which
looked like a leather-covered harness chain in miniature. The first
few times, learning how to do this, you pulled them off.

"I want to hide and talk to you," said Alice finally.

"Come into the hedge," said Adrien, and, since she hesitated for
a moment, "to hide," he added.

The hedge was the secret meeting place for them all. It was
made up of two thick rows of pruned elms and hazel trees inter-
mixed with long tendrils of viburnum, which grew together to
make an arch over a big drainage ditch that was nearly always dry,
with moss-covered sides. Once having squeezed through the wild
boar's lair that provided access, there was a shady, sweet, and secret
silence, a hiding place impenetrable and unknown to the world,
which called for and permitted everything forbidden elsewhere. A
few years earlier, when they were still small and accompanied the
shepherds who passed their time fishing for minnows and loaches,
that's where they had played, happily rebelling by doing the forbidden. Boys and girls proudly stripped naked, offering to view what
was supposed to be kept hidden, sharing in detailed exploration,
triumphantly displaying their differences, abandoning themselves

to the careful touch or the kisses of whoever wished, comparing how they peed, sometimes contenting themselves with mutually and gently holding each other. These rebel games that the adults would have considered impure were, for them, innocent revelation, the exuberant affirmation of their childhood existence. Adrien had passionately loved those moments, guessing in some obscure way that beneath those mysteries revealed so naively was buried a much deeper enigma to which his body did not yet hold the key. At their age now, these amusements were no longer practiced. In their twelve years, they had discovered modesty, and Alice's hesitation brought back a memory, its sweet bliss not completely forgotten in Adrien's heart of hearts.

In the hedge, Alice told her story. The morning of her father's burial, Cécile Brunet had come to get her, a little woman with a pointed nose and no lips, whom she didn't like to kiss because of the hairy wart on her chin. For the first time, she went into the hairdressing salon, where a big wooden armchair with leather cushions sat like a throne, a headrest for shaving facing a mirror with a crack that had been concealed with a painted ivy branch, which covered one whole side of it. In front of the armchair sat a pile of white napkins on a big table with a sink with a faucet in it, beside the pitcher that was used for the hot water. What most struck Alice was a row of different bottles of perfume, near a small dish for lathering the shaving soap and instruments whose uses escaped her, which might have been meant for doing the hair of those young women who wanted curls. Cécile let her smell the perfumes, which she called *sent-bon*. She had even sprayed some on her before plugging in the big upright hair dryer, which Alice put her head into and felt the surprising heat. Germain had returned for lunch. He talked about Fréchaud's burial and named the people who had been there. He didn't say anything about her father. He didn't stop talking all through the meal. They'd eaten radishes, asparagus, a very large roasted rabbit, and a prune tart. Germain poured himself a lot to drink. He had been very eager for Alice to taste his wine. "Oh, leave the little one alone," Cécile had said, "you can see very well she doesn't have the heart to drink wine." After lunch, he had shown her how the clippers shaved hair, he had rolled up her sleeve and passed the nibbling teeth along her arm, and then he had taken her home and kissed her, returning her to her old uncle. She didn't like Germain.

"That's not a secret," said Adrien.

"Yes, it is," said Alice.

She spread her smock out over her knees, took out her handkerchief, carefully undid the knot, and let fall three small black balls, which rolled across the white cloth. Adrien leaned closer, picked up the three lead pellets one after another, and slid them between his fingers.

"They were in the rabbit," said Alice.

"Surely they're from a cartridge."

"I felt them in my teeth and I put them in my pocket. Yes, they're from a cartridge. When Papa made his, he had little sacks full of pellets like that."

"But there's no hunting in the month of May."

"Maybe Germain Brunet went hunting even if it's not allowed."

"But then he went hunting somewhere else. You don't kill rabbits with shotguns in the village. It would make too much noise, it wouldn't be worth the risk. He killed it somewhere else."

"I don't know. But these three pellets were in the rabbit."

"Now that really is a secret," said Adrien. "Now I'm going to tell you mine, my secret, which has really made me scared."

While Alice clutched the lead shot once more in the knot in her handkerchief, he told about the man who was running, about following him, the brown jacket, the discovery of that very cold hidden thing that he had touched, maybe a gun, he said, even though he was certain of it. He hadn't gone back to Champarnaud, but surely it was still there.

"That makes two related secrets," said Alice, "one, maybe a gun, two, a cartridge. Don't repeat them to anyone."

"Not to anyone," said Adrien. "Or else they wouldn't be secrets anymore."

He leaned toward the little girl, kissed her awkwardly on the cheek, near a little curl of light hair, which trembled, and then moved back suddenly as if such gentleness had burned him. She looked at him out of eyes darkened by the light in the hedge and now taking on the iridescent color of the ink at school.

"Is it true that you don't have a father anymore, either?"

"I never had one before," said Adrien. "Now I have Fernand Jublin, but he's not my real father. Maman isn't my real mother, the other, I was too little, I... I don't remember very much."

He didn't dare say that Alice's cheek moved him as much as when those old confused images rose to the surface.

"Are you unhappy?" asked Alice.

"Me? No. That depends. But then, I have Albert and the others, and then I have you, you."

"I am. I'm unhappy," said Alice. "Since my father died, my mother holds me close to quiet me, but it isn't me she's hugging, she doesn't see me, I'm sure of that. My father's taken her partway with him. I don't have a father or mother anymore. Yes, it's tragic."

She looked at Adrien for a long time and made up her mind.

"I want you to stay with me forever."

"Cross my heart and hope to die," said Adrien, rising with happiness.

madame papot

MADAME PAPOT WAS A LITTLE old woman, impeccably dressed in black, right to the satin apron she attached to her bodice using two pins with black heads, and upon which hung her pince-nez from a cord around her neck. A black muslin bonnet, its starched edge ironed into pleats, enclosed her white hair, of which only the beginning of a part could be seen. Her emphysema, which sometimes made her gasp for breath, might have been the reason for the leaden gray tinge of the large, deeply wrinkled face, the graceless nose, the eyes set into deep pockets of yellowish skin, although the look on that face was goodness itself. Seated in her armchair in front of the window through which all she could see was a narrow garden of spindle trees and boxwood, bordered by a wall that a large hazel tree seemed to disrupt, she rested the newspaper on her knees and raised her eyebrows to let her pince-nez fall. She remained pensive and made a gesture to herself, raising and then slowly lowering her hand, which seemed to take pity on all the woes about which she'd just read, and to absolve the poor human species responsible for them.

In her youth, she had wanted to become a teacher, and even though her parents had been afraid of too secular an education, she had gone to a teachers' training college and had taught a class of the youngest children for a brief time. Her father had finally won, marrying her very early to a good match.

Abraham Papot, her husband, was a thin, hard man with strong arms, whose physical body had taken on the forms he gave to his religion, as is the case with certain very devout individuals. His deep faith had led him to become a minister, when his father's death forced him to take over the quarry operations that had made his family rich. Rising at 5 A.M. all his life, he provided the district contractors with raw coal, gravel, very fine white sand made of tiny fossil shellfish that turned to powder at a touch, stones called *de rang* because they were all extracted from the same layer of a little cliff of stratified limestone and were all the same size. Sometimes he helped his workers split the huge blocks to be cut, filling the mining rod holes with powder, or wedging in very dry wood, which only had to be hosed to make it swell up and split the rock.

Abraham's life was pious and austere. When work permitted, he helped Louise cultivate the garden surrounding the house that had sheltered his family from time immemorial. In the large room where they lived and slept, near the back kitchen where Louise did the cooking, he sat in the evening on one of the benches along the table, near the bread drawer, and did his accounts out loud, Louise transcribing them in ink into the large black canvas registers. Under his dictation, Louise wrote out the bills, upon which she inscribed the upstrokes and downstrokes of "debit." On Saturday, Abraham drew out a leather bag from the cupboard, paid his workers, paid himself by giving Louise what she asked for, and then clinked glasses with his men, thanking the Lord for the work accomplished. His rough hands set about counting what increased each week in the bag, and which would one day become a slope of the cleared valley, its various strata revealing new *de rang* stone. Louise filled the soup tureen with slices of bread, over which she poured broth, watching what simmered over the coals in the kitchen grate. Abraham would take the bottle back to the storeroom, after pouring a swig in his hot soup. His only luxury was to eat a lot and to drink wine, which his tall thin body no doubt needed for the effort the quarries demanded. In the evening, Abraham placed the lamp on the fireplace mantel and opened his Bible. For generations, the notes on the fly-leaf had recorded the sequence of great family events, baptisms, and deaths, ending with their marriage.

Abraham loved his wife with a peaceful affection in which the sins of the flesh counted little. He told himself that God had never given them the diversion of children. In their most intimate moments, he had never seen Louise in any way but shrouded in a long nightgown shut tight at the neck, which had a square of cloth at the crotch held closed by two buttons, which when opened exposed the part of the body necessary for sex. Unaware of all she thus missed, Louise nevertheless had experienced some obscure regret. For a long time, she had listened to a ravishing hunger within her, not knowing its object, which the years had extinguished without satiating.

Abraham was dead from having miscalculated the length of a fuse: he was still running for shelter when the explosion had shot out fragments of sharp rock, nearly severing one leg and cutting open the kidneys. Over the years, Louise had slowly grown old, praying often, in a way that had become almost mechanical with age, as if her faith had only been the echo of her husband's and was gradually fading to silence. The lamp had been replaced by an electric bulb, its cord extended to hook onto a thin iron rod hanging from a beam in front of the fireplace, and there Louise read, more often than the Bible, romances inserted in *Le Petit Echo de la Mode:* two pages that you had to fold two times to get eight-page booklets, which she then sewed together, one after another, into a cardboard cover upon which she inscribed only the title, as if, for her, they were all by the same author. Renting the quarries had allowed her to be generous, a trait always surprising in a village where nothing was given without compensation. For a long time she looked after the sick or the widows of poor workers, who received from some unknown source a cartload of wood for the winter or a remnant of fabric. This kindness was limited to humans. From her peasant childhood, Louise had retained a complete indifference with regard to the suffering of animals, whose flesh was only another kind of crop, like the hay in the meadows or the wheat in the fields. When she was a child, she had, like other children, played ball with the toads, dealt savage blows to clumsily mating dogs stuck together tail to tail, or cut the legs off frogs whom she imagined no more alive than the garlic with which they'd be cooked. This insensitivity, which filled some moments on the farms with cold slaughter, con-trasted with Louise's lively affection for a caged turtledove, who announced the rain with a certain kind of cooing.

She had lived alone for a long time. Then her emphysema, com-plicated by frequent warnings from a weakened heart, made it nec-essary for her to remain in her armchair for longer and longer stretches, and to hire a servant. Maria took care of the yard ani-mals, did the gardening, the cleaning, the copperware, the dishes, the big washings twice a year. Each day she used a hazel stick to turn the dry corn shucks that filled the straw mattresses, and she shook the down even in the comforters on the two big canopy beds that sat foot to foot in the back of the room, and that with their curtains opened during the day displayed their richly stitched quilts and eiderdowns. Madame Papot had wanted only to retain control of the kitchen, where she excelled.

She had bound a rabbit by the back feet, hung it to the gate separating the yard from the little garden, pulled out one eye with the point of her knife, and held up the forefeet so that the trickle of blood ran from the socket into the tureen, which she now held in the other hand. The rabbit let out a continuous little piercing cry, so shrill that the dogs howled. Sometimes its jolting made the red trickle leap from the tureen, so Madame Papot had to stand back and hold it with her arms extended to avoid the splattering blood. Then she would say in a low voice and very gently, "Dirty little beast, hold still."

Despite the rabbit's cry, her ears were sharp enough to hear the gate opening very gently behind her and to guess whose quiet steps these were.

"Is that you, Adrien?"

"Yes, ma'am," said Adrien, frozen by what he saw.

"I'm killing a rabbit. There's some vanilla cream left over; ask Maria, she's in the big garden."

"Thank you, ma'am," said Adrien.

He ran behind the house. Half the garden was now lawn. Near the pear and peach trees they had kept only a few squares necessary for the vegetables for the house and along the road, a narrow bed of currant bushes for jam. In big men's shoes, calves bare, Maria turned over a plot for the tomato plants sprawling in a crate that she had slipped into the shade under the wheelbarrow of manure. With each thrust of the spade, the enormous mass of white hair that wreathed her face trembled like a lion's mane. When she saw Adrien, her whole tired face lit up. She planted her spade firmly and opened her arms.

"There you are, my little sunshine," she said, laughing. "I was just saying to myself that I couldn't wait to give you a hug."

Immediately she noticed the little boy's face taut with fear.

"Come!" she said. "I can't bear that cry, either. But she isn't wicked."

She led him above the garden near the two cypress in the cemetery where Abraham and his people were buried. In a curve in the fragrant boxwood hedge, a bench had been provided some time ago to inspire pious memories. Here she sat down and drew Adrien to her. They no longer heard anything. She explained:

"It's for the sauce. She uses the blood. Don't think about it anymore, my treasure. After I've cuddled you, I'll tell you a story."

"Where the wood comes from," said Adrien.

"Okay, ebony and mahogany."

Adrien unbuttoned his collar and stuck his hand under his shirt, drawing out a piece of paper he'd put there so as not to fold it. It was a map of France, very well drawn, with blue rivers and seas, brown hills. He held it toward her.

"This is for you. I made it without tracing."

"It's magnificent."

"The teacher gave me a nine. I only marked two cities, because it was 'River Networks and Mountain Chains.' I marked Paris the capital and Niort the capital of the county."

"It's the county seat."

"I know, but for us, it's our capital. I went there once."

"We are both going to buy a frog in Angelica. We'll ask old Mainson to take us in his cart."

"With Albert?"

"With Albert, if his mother says so. And you, if your mother says so. This summer. We'll take the train. I'll take you to La Rochelle. You must get to know the sea. We can stay with a friend I still have there. My God, how happy it would make me to see it!"

"Will we see boats?"

"Of course! In the port, it never stops. They're lined up nearly nose to tail."

"Will we eat oysters?"

"Why not? Do you like them?"

"I've just eaten them once. There were only three of us in the class who liked them."

It was the custom, about the fifteenth of August, to go to the Aiguillon cove for an outing in wagons in groups of two or three families, and to wade out to the rocks, which were exposed only during the spring tides. There, little oysters, very salty in flavor, were collected, whose shells were then buried in the vineyards to improve the soil.

"Then we will eat oysters," said Maria. "Your map is splendid. I wonder how you can know all that; me, I've forgotten everything.

Look at that, the Lannemezan plateau. I never knew where that was. You draw very well."

"Especially maps," said Adrien.

On one floor of the shed for carts and tools, which he reached using a ladder forbidden to him by Clémence because it was so high, in the midst of firewood left there to dry, he had discovered an empty space. All he needed was a board balanced as a lectern to make an overhead study, a navy admiral's map room, the basket of a balloon, from which you could see to the first drystone walls of the hillsides, and beyond, the thick forests of mahogany, nyangon, or baobab. There, hidden from everyone, watching the farm's comings and goings, he drew lands and seas with a delight that carried him very far beyond his frontiers, coloring in the shores rich with smugglers' coves, basalt caves resonating with the crash of waves where small boats were drawn up onto secret beaches, cliffs aglow with the fires of castaways. It was an adventure to work at drawing the contours of countries, and coloring them added untold, nearly disturbing pleasure. He would have liked to do drawing with Madame Lortier, too, but that was for the girls.

"We'll go around the back," said Maria. "I don't want you to see her skinning the rabbit. I'll put your map in my night-table drawer, that's where I have all my treasures. But what's this! So no hugs today?"

Adrien rushed to her wide bosom, where he hid away like a hare in its den, while Maria showered him with resounding kisses interspersed with gentle words, and then with little tickling pecks that made him burst into laughter. After this tender rage, they remained still, the two of them, Adrien snuggled up in the white flesh of her neck, where his hand played with the tiny folds of skin, rolling them between his fingers, Maria, her lips pressed against the boy's forehead, her face glowing with a dreamy joy. These effusions had become a sort of ritual, and sometimes it was Adrien who wildly embraced his old friend who was beaming as she cried, "You're choking me!" Only once, in his passion, the boy had unbuttoned the top of her blouse and extended his kisses hungrily toward more skin, more softness. Maria had pushed him away almost roughly and her face had suddenly become hard and stern.

"I remembered the name of another tree that used to come in on the boats," she said. "Iroko, I think it grows in an African country called the Gold Coast. You must look for it on the map."

"The Gold Coast? There must be rivers there that transport gold."

"Or mines. Those countries have everything, even diamonds. Ebony, that's another story, that would take too long to tell. I'm just going to give you a nice vanilla cream with some butter cookies; I'll put your map down very carefully, and then I have to get back to my tomatoes."

They got up and went around the house hand in hand. In front of the little door by the boxwood, Adrien stopped.

"The trip to La Rochelle," he said timidly, "did you really mean it?"

Maria hesitated.

"Well, I'm not sure. I can't leave here. But I will try, I promise you that."

"I'll need wine for the stew," called Madame Papot from the back kitchen.

"I'll get it," said Maria.

"A full bottle and a half. This evening we'll drink wine. And get a good bottle. It would be a shame to drink ordinary wine with this rabbit."

Maria sighed: so it was decided, then. She returned with the bottles, uncorked them, and took the little one to the old woman, who was bustling about.

"Are there still coals in the fireplace?"

"Yes, I'm bringing them for you," said Maria.

She got a shovelful of red coals from the fire and slid them into one of the holes in the kitchen grate built into a recess in the wall and lined with patterned earthenware tiles. At the bottom of the hole, on the grate, the old coals were still glowing. Through the openings below, Maria tried to remove the cinders, but they were still too hot.

"Okay," she said, "I'm going to water my tomatoes."

She went out, eagerly took in a deep breath of fresh air, turned from the garden, where the tomatoes had already been watered, and headed for the storeroom. In front of the door, the turtledove hopped about in its cage. She entered the long, partially underground recess leaning against the barn, which covered it with its roof. Weak daylight coming from a hole in the wall covered with wire mesh lit the whole length of empty casks, the mildewed drainage ditches, the old tools with worm-eaten handles, the wood room covered with fine dust from the disintegrating mortar, where the spiders reigned. A wall of boards held the potato harvest. Near the fruit racks and a bottle rack, still hanging from a nail in the beam, fell the string on which Abraham hung his woodcocks. In contrast to this disorder, an orderly niche in the wall had been draped with a cloth, and in it were arranged some cans, a candlestick and matches, a few small bottles, a leather purse. Maria sat down next to it on a low chair, took off her big shoes, put on lighter ones, and remained there for a moment not moving, her hands on her knees. She looked at the row of bottles, the empty place of the ones she had taken. A very old hatred, a cold and humiliated anger resurfaced in this shadowy place where, by a sort of tacit understanding, Madame Papot never entered. "What am I going to do?" she said out loud. She knew that there was nothing else to do but submit, take out the packet of tobacco, roll a cigarette, wait.

It was rare that they drank wine in the house, and it was always Madame Papot who decided it, and it was always in the evening. Maria knew that after only a few glasses a foggy state enveloped her, in which she was suddenly overcome by an irresistible talkativeness she could not control. And she also knew that in the sleep that followed, this unleashing became the cause and the subject of dreams that revealed what she held most precious and most secret, which, upon waking, she retained as a confused memory, clarified here and there with very precise images that cut her to the quick. "Do I talk in my sleep?" she had asked in an artificially light tone, and confirming her fears, Madame Papot had answered, "Oh yes, that happens to you! That happens to you." Always the same, these dreams were at once a pleasure and a torment. There she relived her intimacies with Louis but also with others, and the sad thing was that they became similar. But it was always Louis who sprang up at the beginning of the dream, so real that he didn't seem to belong to sleep. He lay down next to her, she spoke to him, found his body once again under her hands, examined it, explored it with her mouth, devoured it, and then, overcome with a hunger she expressed with a violence, she cried for his caresses, directed and named his movements, entered into those subterranean regions— miry and dazzling, which required brutal and forbidden words— encouraged him, begged him, thanked him, reviled him. Most of the time, even before she had been led to pleasure, the dream became a silvery blank in which vague forms moved about. Just as abruptly, it sometimes happened that Louis's face and body were changed into those of a stranger who swept her along into the heights of love where Louis alone ought to have been master, a stranger who then faded away himself after making wild love to her. Then the vapors of the wine and those of the dream led her into a sleep as still as stone, until the moment when, heavy with images from the night, she rose to help Madame Papot dress. The old woman's look sometimes held a sort of fascinated horror those mornings. On the night table, the glass of water into which, the night before, Maria had counted five drops of digitalis, which had to be taken in case of too-severe heart palpitations, was empty. At the idea that someone had listened to her experiencing her dream, Maria suddenly felt the icy grip of violation, as if whatever still illu- minated existence, not the gestures of love but the state of pure happiness, had been ransacked, destroyed, murdered.

She relit her extinguished cigarette, looking at, without seeing, the perfect sphere of a leek flower gone to seed that she had hung on the wall, so fragile that an imperceptible breath of air set it in motion. Once more she said out loud, "What should I do?" Then, she made up her mind.

Maria set the table, brought in the artichokes and the vinaigrette. Seated facing each other, they ate in silence. With the stew, Madame Papot returned to the subject that had haunted her ever since the double murder had disrupted the village: why these killings? If there was no reason, everyone could feel threatened. That first day, she had asked Maria to clean Abraham's gun, which was kept in the clock beside the pendulum, and which she hadn't wanted to give up to the requisition during the war. Despite her shortness of breath, she had climbed heavily into the attic to find a few old cartridges in the box with the hunting things. The gun now leaned next to the clock, cocked; and thus warded off, her fear had changed to nervousness, but especially to an intense curiosity.

"You won't convince me that there's money beneath it," she said. "If there were, we'd know it. If it were a matter of property, we'd know that, too. So, tell me the reason."

"Eat!" said Maria. "It'll get cold."

"You aren't drinking, my dear; this is good wine, all the same. Have some more."

Maria poured herself another big glass of wine, drank a swallow, took her glass with her into the back kitchen, and came back with it nearly empty.

"An accident," said Madame Papot, "that I can understand. God wills and his wishes are inscrutable. But death at the hands of a murderer, since that's really what he must be called, now that calls for justice on earth."

"Oh! Justice!" said Maria.

"Nevertheless, it's absolutely necessary that he's found. And he'll have his head cut off."

"And pardon, what are you going to do about that? And what if it was a woman?" said Maria for fun.

"Come now! You don't think that!"

"A woman who might have slept with Varadier and whom he was going to leave, who might be getting revenge."

"Oh! That's a horrible thing for you to say!"

"I say many other horrible things, don't I?"

"Of course it's a man, a bad sort."

Maria thought that no doubt she was also a bad sort. She dreamed of La Rochelle, she was at the port, holding Adrien's hand. Luckily the bottle was already nearly empty; she had made that little trip to the back kitchen many times. She saw the rabbit's eye spurting from its socket under knifepoint.

"You've done a fine job with this rabbit."

"Yes, it's good, don't you think? It's the wine that helps it, too. But drink, Maria, your glass is empty."

"You'll end up making my head spin with your wine."

"Bah! Every large pleasure has its small price!..."

Madame Papot wet her lips on the drop of wine she had hardly touched since the meal began. Maria poured herself another big glass, headed toward the kitchen with a dish, lifting her glass to her mouth, and put it down on the table when she returned, full of a wine that had turned very pink. When she had cleared the table, it was still nearly daylight. Madame Papot settled into her armchair with her newspaper, which she rested on her knees, and wanted to ask about Adrien's visit, but Maria avoided the question and talked to herself. The old woman asked for the light, unfolded her newspaper on the table, and read for a moment while Maria closed the shutters, did the bolts, and drew the little curtain across the round window over the ancient sink that now had a faucet and served for washing up.

"My head is spinning," said Maria. "I'm ready to go to bed."

"Mercy, I am, too. Have you covered my little turtledove's cage? Yes? Then give me my drops, my dear."

Maria brought a glass of water from the kitchen and took the medicine bottle and dropper from the night-table drawer.

"Five, no more," said Madame Papot. "To think that this poison is good for me! Digitalis, they used to call it Our Lady's Gloves, you had to be careful of it, and now it's a medicine."

"All the same, it slows down your heart when it's racing."

"My poor heart. I don't know if it'll hold out much longer, the way it pounds."

"Oh hush, you're tough, you're tougher than I am. Tonight my head's all in a fog."

Madame Papot drank, complaining as she did every night of the bitter taste that she had nevertheless gotten used to by now. Maria helped her undress, put on her long nightgown, changed her bonnet after taking out the pins holding her bun, and brought her the footstool thanks to which the old woman, leaning upon Maria's shoulder, heaved herself into the opened bed. With loud sighs, she stretched out.

"God forgive me," she said, "I will say my prayers lying down and during the night. It's just that I don't feel very good. In case I have another spell tonight, Maria, fix me another glass. Five drops, no more," she said while Maria unstopped the bottle.

"No more," said Maria. "There, it's done. Would you like the small lamp?"

"Well, yes. And don't draw my curtains. I'm already suffocating as it is."

Maria lit the night-light, lowering the wick as much as possible. And for a moment the match she was still holding lit her face from below, its features deepened by the shadows, giving her the enigmatic expression of a prophetess before an oracle. She undressed in silence and climbed onto her bed, where she sat down. She heard the old woman say "good night" but didn't respond. She waited. A ray of evening light coming through the crack in the shutters shone on the armoire, its cherry wood glowing darkly. She was afraid. After a moment, she made up her mind. Still seated, eyes closed, she muttered and then called Louis. And even though he appeared immediately and against her will when she was dreaming, now she had to take a moment to conjure him as he was in his glory, danc-ing a waltz, gliding as if pulled by a thread, then, in another image, naked beside her. Closing her eyes, she traced Louis's body with her hands, her mouth, burying herself in the blond comforter, naming and treasuring what she discovered, then she stretched out beside him and called for his gestures, but what, dreaming, was always the same full pleasure now tore her with grief; there was nothing of the lightness and truth of the dreams. She was there on that bed, real and heavy, and the one whom dreams united with her into one flesh was nothing more than an image her hand couldn't touch, disinte-grating as she spoke, and soon her all her grand words of possession embraced that void. Big tears ran down her face as she continued to guide a ghost through dark and secret ways where violence and coarseness had once been ennobling, but where now it all sounded only crude and trite. That wild sweetness that had so often led her out of herself toward dazzlement where some god might have been waiting became, under words deprived of the aura of dream and so describing it without feeling it, an obscene and miserable fornication, just exactly as Madame Papot listened to it as an unprecedented revelation, a stupefying and clearly diabolical discovery, its horror spellbinding her even as she knew she would be punished for it. Through her tears, Maria told herself that for months, in each of her wine-evoked dreams, she had given away an image of her love that defiled it, and suddenly, this felt even worse than the violation of her most intimate treasure, now distorted and reduced to nothing: Madame Papot, petrified there in her bed, was listening to a slut.

Shaken with sobs, Maria fell silent. She might have noticed a noise in the other bed, a body turning over, a hand searching, she no longer knew. She was cold. The silence was suddenly an immense relief to her. She opened her eyes, finding first the thin glimmer of light on the wood of the armoire, and then the limited brightness of the night-light. At that moment, a deep rattle issued from Madame Papot's curtains, the room was filled with a nearly inhuman moaning, which it seemed would not end until a sort of hiccup cut it short. Maria leaped out of bed and ran to the door where the light switch was. First she saw the bed's disorder, a clenched fist that slowly relaxed, the empty glass turned upside down, the sheets thrown back, and then the old woman's face, her terror-stricken expression gradually turning peaceful. She cried, "Madame! Madame!" She shook the inert body violently, its mouth and eyes no longer closing by themselves. Face in her hands, vaguely shaking her head in impossible refusal, Maria kept repeating, "Madame! Madame! My God! My God!" while slow, heavy tears ran down her cheeks. Her wild struggle to defend what she valued more than her life suddenly left her, the death she witnessed surpassing everything, shattering everything. She felt empty, abandoned. In flashes it seemed to her that something of herself was also dead, a powerful bond, maybe an ancient, mute rage, something that, until then, had supported her. Her tears ran like a spring, without a sob. She sat beside the bed, took up the lifeless hand, which was turning cold. A long time later, she pulled herself together, closed the old woman's eyes, and while she bandaged the jaws shut, she painfully saw her again in peaceful images, turning crêpes at the hearth or seated with her Bible in front of the fire, or reading her novels by the window. In the lifeless hands, she placed the little Huguenot cross with its dove and gold tears, Madame Papot's only jewelry, as she would have done according to the custom of what had once been her own religion. She was surprised to hear herself murmuring phrases in which she recognized snatches of the prayers of her childhood. Good and evil, she said to herself, were always somehow mixed.

VIII

lortier

LORTIER WENT OUT BY THE valley gate but, abandoning the little fox and badger trail, followed the path climbing north toward the woods. Like all those going some distance from the village to work in the fields, he had taken his gun, not having too much faith in it himself, more to reassure Mo. It was strange to see the men, sitting on the cloth seat of manure carts, called the *porte-feignant,* weapon across their knees, or planting a field of Jerusalem artichokes, a gun hung from the slats of the wagon. The sight of these weapons, which had nearly all been inspected by the police already, called up a stray, invisible danger, an unknown adversary.

At the top of the climb, on level grass interspersed with orchids, Lortier turned around as always: from this side, the wall of the house, divided by the large portal, allowed for only a view of the roofs and the tower, for which it formed the squat and heavy foundation of a place sure of its strength. A big fire of blazing grass beside the vegetable garden sent out white smoke, above which danced sparks of flame, and this glow recalled the military combat against which this house, with all its many defenses, had held strong. There must have been times, however, when its defenders had fled through the underground passages forming a maze that Lortier had long since given up trying to learn. At the bottom of the well, nearly at water level, a well digger had discovered a bricked-up gallery that dodged the rock and headed toward the fields north before collapsing a dozen meters on. In one of the cellars, a vaulted recess, with a zigzag entrance that could be defended by just one man, disappeared in the same direction and ended in an impassable heap of stone and clay. The ground upon which Lortier freely walked was riddled with hiding places, underground passages, refuges. He wondered if in every inhabited place the same old fear hadn't led men to such mole works, as if the only possible choice was between fighting or fleeing or hiding. On the Nègressauve farm, which he walked toward now, his mind wandering, a servant who was setting a little anvil in the ground under the shed for beating the scythes had come across some tiling, in the middle of which had been set a trapdoor, easily concealed by a bale of hay. Roped together, supplied with picks and lanterns, Lortier and the farmer had descended by a narrow corridor to a kind of natural cave, with a limestone vault supported in spots by crude stonework, mysteriously airy, very big, and empty. By lantern light, they had deciphered on one wall, painted in the blue used for carts, the inscription CRAINS DIEU, FEAR GOD, without being able to tell if this order was a plea from those who trembled for their lives in there, or a threat punishing those above who were torturing and slitting throats.

Before reaching Nègressauve, Lortier turned right into the woods. He wanted to see if thickets had begun to grow back again after last winter's cutting. Even though the noise of the ax sometimes made him sick, he himself had had to give his own wood to make half, as they say, asking that he be left a few sticks for kindling. As a child, he had watched his grandfather cutting alone, then later, keep the split wood and leave the rough wood to the hired help who worked with him, then later still, hire it out to be done, giving up half the wood. Aging, one grew weaker, the opposite of trees. And for a while now, he himself found walking more difficult: his hip hurt, his heart beat too quickly, his mind wandered more and more to ghosts, clung more and more to the hope of days still to come.

The ground changed, became less dry. He crossed a large meadow of short grass prickled with juniper, where bee orchids grew, at the end of which ancient chestnut trees stood guard. Through some irresistible force, for which no heaving could be heard, their enormous trunks had slowly become twisted, over the centuries embracing the earth's rotations, for which they had become the spiraling extension. Behind the chestnut trees, the path went through dense thickets woven with viburnum, where the white hawthorn flowers were already fading and the new growth stopped abruptly to expose the nudity of the oaks that waited, arms raised, rising like sovereigns from the little islands of ferns and the small copses. Lortier took a grassy, muddy path that the May sun hadn't yet dried, where his steps were muffled. He stopped in a very open spot where the wild boars had turned up the ground and, as he did so often, leaned against a tree trunk, waiting to become the forest himself. He didn't hear any birds, except sometimes the sharp cry of the jays and, very far off, the stubborn determination of a woodpecker. No wind moved the new leaves, strong and gleaming, their outlines softening with the distance in such a way that, far off, they seemed drawn on the joyous blue of a sky crossed by the wind-filled sails of clouds. Nearer to him, small, still-slender beech trees were sending out their scalloped leaves; he took one by its sculpted edge, which he munched on like a deer. Across from him, an old indestructible oak, one whole side of which had been split open and charred by lightning's fiery ax, was leafing out on its still-vigorous side, while at its foot, other oaks only as tall as a finger and with just two or three leaves forced their way irresistibly from the ground. Lortier listened, not moving, to the formidable energy of the forest's rebirth. He also came here when it snowed, when the long shadows and cold light of winter transfixed the gray ruddiness of those leaves the oaks seemed to hold on to with all their strength, when the highest bare black branches of the beeches traced a fine network of cracks across the porcelain sky. And in the frozen forest, enclosing all that had chosen its protection, the mist of a mysterious breathing sometimes passed, erasing everything, and Lortier was no longer sure if it might not be his own breath washing away all the colors.

In the summer, in the trembling air of an opened oven door, when the underbrush, dying for water, became brittle and crackling, angry storms often rumbled over the trees, and sometimes a few drops of eagerly swallowed rain escaped from their engorged clouds. Lortier waited there as flashing hieroglyphs of lightning were inscribed in the clouds' blazing copper, and as finally the streams of rain he offered his face to filled the steaming forest. But for him as he aged, nothing compared to the moment he experienced there now, to the rebirth of spring, to these little oaks, just born and rich with their two leaves, which would later offer themselves to the thunder's flaming graffiti. This place knew only the seasons, ignoring the time that disappeared, whirling in its vertiginous silence. Resting against the rough tree trunk, a false hermit loving nothing other than the eternity of the trees, he imagined that the forest allowed itself to be penetrated only in solitude, but once conquered and understood, it revealed to him a sense of utmost existence, nearly a wisdom, and taught him a generous sympathy that led him to love people more than to avoid them.

A long time later, Lortier began walking again toward the little cut that belonged to him. From a distance, he saw the treeless spot lighting up the forest, and at its edge, in the light from a gap in the foliage, stood outlined the perfect candelabra of a little pine in all its grandeur, bearing its very bright new growth like lit candles. Behind it, a swell of proliferating shoots grew out from the stumps. These signs were enough for him. He reconsidered the itinerary of his walk. Often he chose to go on to Fontmaillol, with its small mysterious grassy amphitheater, surrounded by ash, a reminder that no doubt it had once been a sacred place, the white stream of a spring gushed, thick as a wrist, between two rocks, one of which had been hollowed out into a trough and spilled into a thick current of water running over the slopes to rejoin the river at the lower bridge, a long way off. A few wild vines, whose grapes must have been used as offerings, formed a strange crown over these rocks.

Lortier loved this inspired place, this inexhaustible water into which he had once hung a line for fun and caught an enormous eel, and he had never known if it had come from the rock or was returning to it. And since it was caught by just the edge of its snout, he had unhooked it and returned it to the spring where it might have been guardian. But if it was easy to go to Fontmaillol by the other side of the valley, from where he was, he would have to leave the path, cross the fields, go through some other woods, and follow the high wall surrounding the grounds of a noble old house with turrets and weather vanes, with no other houses close by, long uninhabited until a family with a daughter who barked had retreated from the world there. Behind the wall, you often heard those hoarse barks, which sounded like a large dog or a startled deer, or little yelps that sounded like complaints. The parents only went out on Sunday for mass. The baker who brought them bread and deliveries said that the young girl was as beautiful as an angel, dressed like a princess, but as soon as she saw him, she looked up toward the sky, extended her neck, and let out a howl like a wolf. Many times Lortier had heard and, even though he walked noiselessly, perhaps caused those wild cries that tied his stomach into knots. He no longer passed that way except when necessary. The spring would have to wait for another day.

His gun felt heavy, like after a long day of hunting; his shoulder was weaker, too. The unloaded weapon and the two cartridges in his pocket made no sense. If there was a mad murderer, he would shoot without warning, and besides, Lortier didn't believe there was one. He decided that, as heavy as it was, his gun was not going to make him go back. He would reach the stubble fields by the Outremont, cross the stream over the ford between the two bridges, and go up to say hello to the basket maker. That was a long way around, but since, for some time now, he was always tired, this walk wouldn't change anything much. What exasperated him in his old age wasn't so much the way time was running out as the way his body didn't obey him, always falling short of what he asked of it. It was that this slowing down would only get worse. His occupation had let him live in very remote times; from carved stones, the ends of bones or paintings, he had tried to imagine the movements, the rituals, the fears of unknown beings. He had discovered them dead, sometimes resting inexplicably, already, on the pollen from ancient flowers. But he had never imagined them old.

"That's how it is," he said to himself. He was old, and that made him more impatient than morose. And although others hadn't noticed, except for Mo, who saw everything about him immediately, his character was also changing, becoming more taciturn, more solitary, perhaps more indulgent, too, reconsidering, though in secret, the growing importance children were coming to have for him. He smiled because he would have to say more passionate, too, riveted to Mo, hopelessly mingled with her. Because, if in the past this dependence had been painful, he really had to admit that now she illuminated his days, smiling to himself with pleasure, yes, more passionate. This idea made the gun feel lighter. Arriving above Champarnaud, he descended, found the animals' trail, and all at once came upon the great open space of the valley, which made him take a deep breath, as is so often the case with a commanding spot. Below him, at the Pont-Bertrand washing place, two women kneeled on their wooden kneeling pads were doing their wash; one of them wrung out and beat her laundry on her board, the other had laid a large white cloth in the stream of water, where it floated and swelled. Lortier recognized Elodie Russeille, a young, strong Nausicaa whose arms seemed as white as her laundry, and Maria's mane of hair, white, too. A third woman, whom he couldn't see very well, stacked twisted sheets onto an openwork cart. In such dry air, the noise of the beater hitting the board rose toward him with surprising clarity, and a few words of Elodie's animated conversation, although so far off, were quite distinct. He heard Maria's great laugh, which made him smile happily. The heart attack that had carried off Madame Papot had plunged Maria into a state of distraction that led her to come and go without reason. When she came out of a sort of mute anxiety, she accused herself of not having taken care of the old woman well enough, and of being the cause of her death. She had walked alone in tears ahead of the men when the coffin had been carried to the end of the garden, where the pastor had read the Twenty-third Psalm, "When I walk through the valley of death." Since Maria found the meadow flowers prettier than the snapdragons and gillyflowers from the massifs, she covered the tomb with big bouquets of Queen Anne's lace, meadowsweet, and wild gladiolus, and even though these gestures would no doubt displease the Huguenots buried there, she had planted a border of wood sorrel all around it.

She had packed up everything to leave, though she still didn't know where to go, but near the village in any case because of Adrien. Mo had already offered her a room when a disturbing summons from the lawyer had arrived, and she had asked Lortier to accompany her. The mayor was there. She didn't dare sit down. Dumbfounded, incredulous, she heard the lawyer read the will Madame Papot had recorded in the beautiful handwriting that once had inscribed the "debit" on Abraham's bills or the titles on the covers of her little novels. Everything in the savings bank was divided between the Protestant Religious Association of Celles-sur-Belle and the charity office of the village, which was given ownership of the quarries and the woods, making it responsible for doing the cutting and distributing of wood and firewood to the poor. The rent from the quarries would be allocated to the charity office. The village became owner without usufruct of the house, for which Maria had usufruct of property and goods for the rest of her life. Maria was given ownership of a field subject to respecting the current lease and a parcel of woodland for firewood. The mayor was certain that the bequest would be gratefully accepted by the municipal council. While waiting to take possession, Maria would continue to enjoy all the property over which she was given usufruct.

Stammering, she had thanked the lawyer and the mayor, her fingernails digging into Lortier's sleeve. Once outside, as if over-whelmed by her new and surprising condition, she had walked silently next to Lortier, who rejoiced out loud:

"Do you realize, Maria? Here you are with a roof over your head, a garden, a field, all yours! I know that field, it's Caillon who grows wheat there. With the first rent, you'll control the rights, you'll be free, you'll be your own mistress! Glory to Madame Papot!"

"Do you believe in God?" Maria had suddenly asked.

Astonished, Lortier had answered that he didn't believe in churches, that he didn't really know very well what he believed in, he felt as though he were a religious being with no faith. Maria had nodded her head. Later, she had only murmured, "I'll take Adrien to La Rochelle."

And as she left Lortier, after having thanked him, she had spoken this surprising sentence:

"Maybe sometimes God wants to punish the just and compensate the sinner."

Lortier had witnessed her humility there. Maria had paid visits to all her neighbors as if she had moved into a new life. She had done a big cleaning, a laundry that she had come to rinse out at the washing place with the others.

The gestures that Lortier saw from above, the lively talk and laughter, were for him small proof, but proof, of the invisible order of the world hidden under the confused chaos that masked it. He descended happily across the stubble fields, where the grass was very slippery, and he suddenly saw himself as a boy clinging to the two feet of a washboard stolen from the pile the women left at the washing place, lying on this sled smooth with soap and hurtling down the stubble field at a speed that enthralled him with pleasure and terror. Sometimes it happened that you smashed into the wall at the bottom, but you carried the board back up, you turned it around to grab on to the feet, and once more you threw yourself into that speed until your legs refused to climb up again. This image was so precise and so cheerful that he forgot his tiredness, crossed the meadow where, here and there, a few clumps of sainfoin raised their pink blossoms, and cleared the ford that the ancient collapse of riverbank walls had provided. On the other side, a steep path rose diagonally and he climbed it slowly, sometimes stopping to smile at his past agility, as if on his shoulder he carried a washboard transformed into a sled rather than a gun. Finally, set off from the foliage of the trees, he saw the tarred roof of the trailer belonging to Emile Baromé, called l'Anguille, called la Musique, and to his wife, Malvina, basket makers.

The dog let out two resounding barks and came, wrinkling his muzzle in pleasure, to rub up against the legs of Lortier, who stumbled over pieces of an old beam rotting in the ivy. The trailer was permanently lodged on a level terrace where only an old half-ruined well remained of a very ancient structure, a few of its stones forming bumps among the brambles. In front of it, a very tall plane tree, from which, in the autumn, the village women carefully gathered leaves for drying their cheeses on, marked the fork in the path that Lortier had taken and the valley road. Two climbing rosebushes seemed to hold up certain boards in the sides of the trailer, still painted a peeling green; others had cracks stuffed with newspaper. Over the door, its steps reinforced by bricks, the name VILLA VIOLETTA had been painted in beautiful round letters and bordered with flowers. Between the wheels, a sort of henhouse, where three dwarf hens and a rooster pecked, sat next to two wire cages out of which gleamed the red eyes of rabbits. In the clearing between the trailer and the plane tree, near a propped-up donkey cart strangely tarped on three sides right to the ground, next to tubs where osier and hazel branches soaked, Emile sat on a saddle, working. At the dog's bark, he raised his head and made a friendly gesture with his hand, his whole face so furrowed it seemed swollen, smiling, his eyes very black and lively under a forest of eyebrows and short bushy white hair. At the same time as Lortier approached, Malvina appeared, short and stooped, at the top of the steps under the awning, dressed in a sort of white shapeless camisole, her bare feet in men's shoes, braiding her long gray hair, and retaining a hint of beauty in her milky skin creased by very fine wrinkles, like a winter apple.

"So why don't you ever warn me!" she cried. "If I'd known, I would have gotten dressed and washed up?"

"How would you like me to warn you other than by coming?" said Lortier, laughing.

"Don't listen to her," said Emile, shaking his hand. "An old mule deserves a golden bit, but there's not much gold around here. It's always a blessing to have visitors, and it will be an even greater one when you've given me my hundred sous."

That was the ritual. Lortier had supplied himself with the two coins that he now pulled happily from his pocket.

"What say!" cried Emile to his wife. "It's already divided up. There you go! Ask and it shall be given, *audaces fortuna juvat*, fortune smiles on the daring, as the ancients said."

They really did divide the price of each basket, of each demi-john re-covered in wicker, in such a way that when one of them offered the other a bottle of wine or a box of cookies, it was a true gift. Moreover, they both worked wicker so skillfully, it was impossible to distinguish one's work from the other's, which was what justified their agreement.

"I won't make you come in, you'd only see our poverty," said Malvina, disappearing into the trailer.

"First thing," said Emile, drawing up another saddle next to his own. "This is the Baromé republic here, French territory, guns remain at the entrance. What the hell are you going to do to me with that contraption, like all the other jokers I see going by here?"

"Oh, you know why."

"It's exactly because I know why that I also know it doesn't do any good. Put that blunderbuss in the cart. There! Now sit down peacefully. Second thing..."

"I know," said Lortier, getting out his tobacco pouch.

"My word, what a pleasure to be among well-brought-up people. Don't mind if I do," he said as he filled his pipe. "You know what they say, the one near the fire gets warm. I profit from you like a soldier enjoying his seized lodgings. But I also have something for Madame Lortier; Malvina. Bring the little basket, please."

She had put a green-and-white-striped blouse over her camisole, a little faded under the arms. With surprising agility for her age, she came down the steps to offer a little cup in the form of a nest, braided in bands of seven strands so skillfully put together you couldn't see where the interlacing began or ended.

"For putting rings in," she said, graciously making a bow.

"Or small change," said Emile.

"How can you braid anything so fine!" exclaimed Lortier.

"That's our art," said Malvina.

"It's wild elm," said Emile, "the one called Saint John's elm, which has little, very regular shoots. You dry it very gently, and then you soak it until it creases under the thumb, but without letting it get moldy. I prefer it to cane, the wood has a cleaner color."

They were satisfied. They had left at the beginning of April with the little donkey cart full of their winter's work, the dog, the rooster, and three hens, but without the rabbits, which they had eaten. They stopped at the entrance to villages, near a well. They covered the cart shafts with a canvas under which they slept, taking shelter from showers under the cart. Malvina changed shirts out in the open. They addressed each other as *vous* when they quarreled, but in the evening, after making the village rounds, in front of their fire, Emile pulled out of the bric-a-brac what he called his country violin, an instrument he'd made from an old oval wooden box that might have been an opera hat box, the mahogany arm from an easy chair that he'd carved, and a yew wood bow with a peg allowing him to tighten the horsehairs. Only the strings were real strings. He played "by ear," not knowing the music, but with a very true ear and the agile fingers of a basket maker. He played marches or songs or slow tunes invented with a tenderness that produced a half smile on his face, suddenly ennobled by the music. The violin had a shrill, muffled tone that Malvina listened to, smiling dreamily, sitting straight as a queen on an upside-down pail. Later, he had been able to get himself a real violin, which was kept carefully hidden in a secret cranny of the trailer. And that had become his second occupation. In the black, well-ironed costume he put on only for these occasions, wearing a black hat, holding under his chin the real violin sporting a cascade of ribbons, he walked in front of wedding parties playing nonstop those lively melodies he remembered or invented, which, in the evening, made the company dance. And since Malvina took care of the costume, they divided the profits from the music as well. But that had nearly come to an end now, since wedding parties had gramophones and even radios. And the war had disrupted everything.

"If I had still had hazel baskets," said Emile, "I would have been able to sell them all. I had the buyers. They liked them because hazel's so white. We sold everything."

"And since we're rich," said Malvina happily, "we went on a spree, a real corked wine that stains your bread a good red. Each to his own bottle."

"And since I believe I've still got one of them left," said Emile, "let's offer a toast."

He pulled out a bottle hidden in the tub under the osiers, and Malvina let out a little surprised laugh. She leaped into the trailer and returned with a tray holding three glasses and a plate of butter cookies, which she set on the ground. Lortier was reminded of the ancestral ceremonies for meeting, the exchange of gifts, the shared food and wine. Clinking his glass, he told himself that what he always came here to find was this vision of a kind of freedom. His hosts were free of ties, detours, were free from the history that had starved but spared them during the war, strangers to the affairs of the world, deaf to its unbearable noise because of their singularity, free even of the village's burdensome envy, its petty jealousies, its bitter tongue, its endless calculations. Seated on his wooden saddle, drinking strong, heavy wine, he felt happy and calm, restored to an ageless simplicity that gave him back a sort of innocence.

"They're beautiful, these trips, still I'm always happy to return to the Villa," said Malvina, motioning to the trailer. "It's easier for my cooking."

"What's that you're saying!" said Emile. "You cook outside on the fire here, too."

"But I'm at home."

"Look at this home!" said Emile, gesturing wide to the square of hard earth cluttered with utensils, where new baskets were drying before red coals. "*Cuique suum stercus bene olet,* each of us thinks his own shit smells sweet, as they used to say when I wanted to become a priest."

"You, become a priest?" said Lortier, amazed.

"But I was there," said Malvina. "Can you see him as a priest, my artist?"

A light brightened Emile's face.

"When you're the last in a procession of boys, among the poor hired hands in Gâtine," he said softly, "and when you succeed at the catechism, the priests take you, by force. That takes care of the family. Let us say that afterward, I chose to worship the Lord in the form of one of his creatures."

Malvina straightened her bent back and her eyes suddenly shone with youth.

"He lost himself in the religion of me," she said with a happy smile. "And believe me, he certainly knows his prayer book."

"That doesn't stop me from saying my other prayers sometimes, to thank the good Lord for having taught me that very religion."

"Even if we are always running after a few cents, we know well enough that the good Lord has made us rich, don't we, Emile?" she said, extending her glass toward the offered bottle, and Lortier suddenly saw the beam in their eyes as they met, their two old faces responding to each other with a joy intact.

"Let's drink to that wealth," said Lortier. "I know it, too. To your health, both of you."

Emile took the extended tobacco pouch, got out his pipe, changed his mind, and rolled a cigarette.

"Well, that's not everything," he said. "Now it's your turn. Last time we got no farther than Peru, to the digs you did up there."

He had to tell about it. Emile was curious about everything, he delighted in expanding his world, he approached unknown countries with a passion, wanting Lortier to describe the landscapes, the animals and flowers, the houses, the customs. Present life interested him more than the riddles Lortier and his team drew from the earth where they had been sleeping for thousands of years. Nevertheless, when Lortier mentioned the times when, perhaps before they knew how to make pottery, men had coated wicker baskets with clay to harden them in the fire, he had been deeply moved to discover the breathtaking ancestry of his craft. He spoke of it often since, saying that his movements were ageless, that all you needed was a sharp blade, a boxwood cleaver, and the materials the good Lord had made, as much now as in prehistoric times. And the idea that he was the heir to a technique so ancient filled him with pride.

Lortier talked about the painted rock, the bone needles, the skeleton of a woman with an elbow made arthritic nine thousand years earlier from tanning, then about the shepherds' enclosures, the herds of sheep and llamas protected from the condors and pumas, the hellish wind, and under the thatched ichu grass roof, after the intense heat of the day, the nocturnal cold, hardly kept at bay by the weak flame from dried animal droppings mixed with peat. Emile listened, fascinated, as if he were watching those images from the high Andes plain superimposed over the huge plane tree and erasing the peaceful foliage of the Poitou ash trees. When the bottle was empty, Lortier rose, Emile seemed to awaken from a daydream, and Malvina straightened up on her seat with the kind of smile that follows the end of a story and gave a deep sigh. Lortier, happy, took his gun from the cart and put the strap over his shoulder.

"And you, you walk around with your bird gun after seeing all that?" said Emile.

"It's the times that call for it."

"Well, if it was me, if I'd gone to those countries, I wouldn't be afraid of anything anymore. Leave that gun with me and grab a good stick."

"It reassures my wife. Even so, hasn't a murderer passed this way?"

Emile laughed to himself, a little mocking laugh.

"I know, I know. I tell you, I've never hurt anyone, except once, a long time ago, in Rabistoque, when I was attacked. Rest his soul, he died all alone in a ditch, laid low by the bottle. But I have two good eyes."

"Here, in the open air," said Malvina, "you live without malice and you see everything."

"Yes, that's true! Look at the bend in the road over there, what do you see?"

"A field and apple trees."

"What else?"

"Ah! You mean the little stone path water runs down in winter?"

"That's it! Between those two lovely hedges. And the nearest hedge has a big gap in it, at least thirty meters. And when someone secretly passes along that little path, you see them through that gap."

"Okay, I give up."

"Oh! I'm not saying anything! And careful, not so loud! I have enough heat as it is, let's not jump from the frying pan into the fire. But when you see a man passing stiff as rail with the hunting pocket of his jacket all lumpy? Or when you see a man passing with that same pocket, but limping as if he had a wooden leg? Listen, a rifle butt, that can always be hidden in the back pocket, but the barrel, that doesn't fold, that slides under the jacket between the shoulders or in a pant leg. Not seen, not caught."

"But you do see," said Malvina with a smile that suddenly gave her pointed face the cruelty of a bloodthirsty weasel.

"But mum's the word here. All that for a bit of advice: put away your peashooter. It won't happen again, in my opinion."

"Good!" said Lortier. "If I understand correctly, you haven't told me anything?"

"Exactly."

"Even so, I'm left with something to mull over. Thanks for the pretty cup, thanks for the wine."

"Thanks for the story," said Malvina.

Lortier climbed as far as the plane tree, turned around, and waved to his open-air hosts, who stood side by side. "Death alone will separate them," he said to himself, and this trite phrase struck him as so marvelous that he was suddenly choked up with emotion. "Okay, let's go! Here I am turning into a crybaby!" He walked more quickly, forcing himself to think about Emile's last secret. He would have preferred not to know it: a man had gone down into the valley hiding a gun. But he, Lortier, didn't know the name of that man. You could only guess that to pass that way, he had to come from the Bastière, and besides Lortier wasn't very interested in all that. He only would have liked to see justice done for little Alice's sake, and also for the simple sake of justice itself, even though the great injustice didn't lie in the unknown culprit's impunity.

He hesitated, left the road, and took the path hemmed in by drystone walls above the stubble fields that ran along the end of the gardens extending from the houses. Thus, he avoided passing the one where his grandparents had lived, a house of happiness now long dead, which perhaps he had betrayed as well. He had no need to see it, he knew it by heart, he still knew which door was hard to open, which step creaked, and, even though this was perhaps the hardest memory to call up, which scent marked his room, converted from an old loft, where the slightly fermented grain had permeated the walls and floor with a deep odor that hinted of bread. He had only to think of the house for a sequence of unconnected images to arise, his grandfather whistling, talking to his bees, his grandfather taking out his glasses from their wooden case to make his cartridges or to tie the net, knot after knot; his grandmother, in the fluted and ribboned white bonnet Poitou women wore, taking him along to mass on Sunday, where the sacred bread was sometimes brioche donated by Madame de Cherves, his grandmother reading out loud to herself with feeling, stumbling through the newspaper's account of international politics, or in the evening murmuring her prayers while undressing for the night, or even later, when he was grown up, climbing laboriously up to the second floor just to ask him if he thought there would be war. These places had revealed to him the age-old adaptation of one form of life to one environment, a skillful way of living with nature and, to a certain extent, of venerating it by submitting to it. He imagined that at the school he would pass in a moment, where his father had passed on to him his own passion for learning, he had discovered at nearly the same time the law, a moral code, a kind of stubborn pride that could only be called virtue. What had he made of all that? He didn't know a wretched thing, not a thing anymore, maybe he wouldn't know anything right up to the end, maybe he would discover that he hadn't been worthy of it, or maybe this was simply all there was, this was the inexhaustible source to which he had needed to return more and more often.

Thus creased by memory, the borders of his life drew together, his childhood and the present touching each other.

He recognized the wall where he had helped his grandfather set the trap in which the martens, drawn to the houses in winter, were caught. The gloves, the trap, and its chain, they all had been smoked over a broom fire. Only the egg resting on the palette showed above the deceptive dead leaves in the cavity on the crest of the wall. The little wild creature was too concerned about keeping its feet clean to choose a way around the wall. Above, Lortier noticed the familiar roof that now housed a dry, lipless, pointed-nosed old widow who spied on everyone, knew everything, guessed which girls were pregnant before they grew round, in whom others' misfortune awakened a feverish delight: Zélie Madron, called la Mailloche since the day when, worming her way to the bedside of a girl suffering a cruel death in childbirth, she had smiled and said softly, "She really must have known that the maul was bigger than the handle."

"The devil take her," he said to himself. The house wasn't made for spitefulness, and he secretly thought that it ought to reject Zélie, tear up her smock with the keys to the doors, smash her head on the fireplace mantel, turn her cauldrons upside down, her frying pan oil, make the steps slippery under her feet. Lying dormant in the stillness of things was a mysterious power that could render them friendly or hostile. They conspired to bring about good or bad fortune, which was customarily called chance. Even if, by unknown black spells, Zélie had forced the house to serve her evil purposes for the time being, one day the house would be stronger than her deviltry and would chase her out, reclaiming its essential nature as a place favorable to goodness. Lortier laughed to himself at these crazy ideas, but a very small voice, also laughing, said, "Yes, but still...?" The seeds planted by the stories of long ago, the adventures of the four Aymon brothers and Merlin the magician, or the castles fallen from the smock of Melusine, the fairy serpent, had left in him shoots still so strong that he would have welcomed the supernatural without fear, since he already believed in the invisible in the forest.

He made himself keep walking, climbed back up through a garden alleyway to the empty village that, at this time of day, was busy taking care of the herds, and passed by the Jublin farm where Adrien didn't appear. Lortier liked this reserved child who was curious about everything and especially about discovering the world. He found in him a lively sensibility. He was surprised by Adrien's rapt attention for the large engraved reproduction of *The Shepherds of Arcadia,* by his long examination of the paintings in the parlor, by his interest in the objects decorating the house. The little fellow came to Puypouzin more and more often after school, when he didn't have to watch the herd, and Lortier was surprised to notice that between four and five o'clock he himself stayed at home most of the time, as if he waited for this visit, which was generally passed in responding to questions from this boy for whom Mo always had some little treat. He continued along his way, waved to Paulus, the cobbler, whose orthopedic shoe creaked with each step, like a mouse in a trap. He walked past the quiet school where memories that he had pushed back jostled with each other, although he welcomed the one of his father's good face, and turning toward the valley came face to face with the Cherves domain.

The big house was closed up, and its state of disrepair empha-
sized its isolation even more. A shutter hung from its hinges, the
grass was taller than the first-floor windowsills, and, eaten away by
rust, the border of sheet metal around the awning was falling down
over the double stairway of the entrance. The grounds had been left
to go wild and the windowless greenhouse opened to all the winds.
Everyone was dead, maybe Nedège, too, who had never been able
to give René a son. Monsieur Méhus de Cherves was so proud of
his lineage that he had killed off at a young age, on the genealogical
family tree, the one ancestor who had actually died at Valmy in the
Republic's ranks. To those who knew, he said, "There's no tree so
high that it doesn't have a few low branches." He was so exquisitely
polite that it was hard to tell if his manner masked great refinement
or profound disinterest. But one evening at dinner when the marchioness mentioned an Indian silk scarf she'd seen at Celles that she
liked, he asked her to excuse him from lunch the next day, as he
wanted to go check on his wood. Celles was fourteen kilometers
away; he walked all day, and that evening the silk scarf was under
his wife's napkin. Nothing remained of all that, nothing. Not Clovis
who took care of the horses and said to Monsieur René, "There's
no lack of masters like you and jackasses like me," nor old Jamine,
the cook who came there when she was fourteen because her parents couldn't pay their farm rent, who adored Madame and was no
doubt more loved at Cherves than in her family, who had never
received a cent in wages and whose only treasure was a boxwood
snuffbox in the form of a coffin with a secret lock.

Dead, all of that, finished, erased, wiped out, buried! The house
done in, eaten by the grass, the untiring, insatiable, triumphant

grass. The grounds would be divided into parcels, already the beautiful Protestant chapel had been destroyed to make a shelter for
carts. Finished. Everything dies, the Cherves family cemetery itself
would die, like the tombs with the names worn off that are dug up
to extend the fields. You, too, Lortier, don't forget. Your old childhood house is already dead. No regrets, never. The past is never better. It's enough to quietly and peacefully remember it.

He descended along the wall of the grounds, took the rocky little
path that cut across to the lower bridge, and soon came again upon
the imposing silhouette of Puypouzin, heightened by the cliff, against
the blue of a sky streaked with swifts in flight. At the bridge, he
took the path that climbed back up to the stubble fields, stopped to
catch his breath, and, looking up, discovered the valley already
growing dark, transformed by evening. Patches of fog were forming
here and there, like strange smoky cloth, giving the distant meadows
the barbaric look of a country in flames. Over to the east, the sky
had the iridescent pallor of trembling mauve water being slowly
swallowed up by an invisible abyss as it fell vertiginously into night.
Lortier said to himself that his days had been woven so tightly he no
longer saw the thread; they seemed like a smooth and uniform fabric
over which was inscribed by chance, like the swifts' transient flights
across the sky, some moments in life that chose to spring forth
before erasing themselves. All the pasts that he'd been taught, even
the one of his own species, which he had so stubbornly sought to
discover, had succeeded in making a successor of him. Only his own
past escaped this construction. The fabric had so many meanings, he
saw neither borders nor fringes there; the periods of time were

blurred by indistinct and changing places with no link between them. Except that the warp of this cloth was that irrefutable and mysterious core of identity that united all the ages of his life. He could only distinguish the moments illuminated by happiness, suddenly springing back to life in a way that surprised him, or, obedient to the given order of memory, inscribing themselves in fiery embroideries. He knew that he had nourished death with these timeless moments, that he had thrown them to it to keep it at a distance, as you throw bloody pieces of meat to wild animals to keep them away. Taking advantage of all those days in which he had nevertheless learned, felt, and experienced, but that had forever disappeared from his memory, it was approaching, stealthily regaining lost ground. He had to endlessly appease those devouring jaws with the memory of happiness, or with happiness itself, toward which he now began walking again. Mo was waiting for him. The terrace lamp had been lit. Lortier felt very tired, a tiredness older than that of his long walk, but all that counted for him now was the limitless future of his love for this woman who had lit the lamp for his safe return.

the gun

FROM HIS HIDEOUT SURROUNDED by firewood up in the cart shed, Adrien observed the yard like a lookout examines the horizon. The chickens fussed noisily about the manure while Sirène slept in the sun at the foot of the straw pile. Fernand and André had left with the horse and the mower to cut the red clover in the Alaric field, and Clémence had disappeared under the low roofs with an armful of nettles to chop up for her ducks. He was alone to watch over this world and he was bored, his lessons learned, his composition finished. In the privacy of his hiding place, he had copied for class the map of coastal rivers, then for his own pleasure he had enlarged the map of the Sèvre, where the marsh became a fine network of blue lines representing the reaches, the canals, and the channels called the conches. On the banks, he had drawn poplars, a flat-bottomed boat, an eel net, and a little fellow fishing, his pole upright, the line stretched taut by a fish whose head was emerging from the green water. Near the little fellow, he had written, "Me."

For Adrien, nothing compared to the Sundays when Fernand woke him early to take him to the marshes to fish. Already the day before, the preparations themselves were a kind of holiday. Big potatoes were cooked and old bread was soaked to shape into balls for bait, wheat and hemp seed were boiled up in water, the little

red worms from the manure pile and the earthworms from the garden swarmed in the dirt in their box, rods and lines were prepared,
hooks attached with complicated knots on roots as fine as hairs.
They arrived at the marsh at sunrise. It was cool and the water
seemed dark and very mysterious. It moved in great waves when
they disturbed it by stepping into the boat, and they sat down noiselessly on the two boards in the back.

Fernand always fixed his line at the last minute. He chose his
line and his weight according to the spot, the grass at the bottom,
the color of the water. On those days, he rediscovered in himself an
unsuspected preciseness and vivacity. He was happy, and he was
especially happy to see Adrien untangle his line all by himself and
bait his hook with a grain of wheat. He laughed with delight when
the boy caught a big roach. He showed him how to unhook it with
a disgorger without damaging it. Speaking quietly, he taught him
how to tell a bream's bite from a tench's, or he taught him how to
tire a big fish using a very fine line without breaking it. Everything
became remarkable, as though enchanted, the silence suddenly
accompanied by a rat diving in or chub leaping, the flatness of distant noises reflected by the water, the ripples breaking up the trembling reflection of the poplars through which the cork, carried by
the current, cut a fine line before blending into the marbled image
of the white sky. In the net attached to the seat gleamed, from time
to time, the glittering scales of the roaches, the perch's rainbows,
and the velvety bronze of the tenches. The scent of tar from the
boat mixed with the odor of mint and cut grass.

Seated on either side of the boat, almost with their backs turned
to each other, they exchanged few words in very soft voices, but in

these whispers interspersed with long silences, something very precious united them, which Adrien felt strongly. Sometimes Fernand,
in a hushed voice, spoke of his childhood, revealed to Adrien, nearly in secret, the memory of his grandfather, whom he had adored.
His grandfather was a sorcerer, a dowser. He removed warts and
cured burns. He circled them slowly three times, moving in the
direction opposite the sun's and muttering certain words, which
died with him, and then he said out loud, extending his hand over
the wound, "Fire, lose your heat, as Our Lord lost his color in the
garden of the olive trees," and the burn stopped hurting. The old
man had only ever seen olive trees in his Bible, but he thought the
tree was magic. Likewise magic was the Yule log, which was supposed
to burn for three days before it was reduced to coals by striking it,
and the number of coals foretold the future abundance of fish. One
of these coals was put under the bed as a protection against thunder,
and this was the coal that relit the Yule log the following Christmas.
The night of Christmas itself was enchanted. This was the night
when the animals spoke and during which you had to take care not
to enter the stables so as not to draw death into the house. A servant
his grandfather knew had gone to check his animals despite the pro-
hibition, and one of the cattle had said, "What will they be doing
next week?" Another answered, "Why, you know of course, they'll
be putting our master in the ground!" His grandfather told how the
man who had built his childhood house had walked around it
spilling, drop by drop, the blood of a black hen slaughtered before
the altar to attract the prosperity of the Pleiades, then called la
Poussinière, on the chest of Taurus. He swore that under the stone
of the door sill, an egg had been buried in the clay as homage to the

power that makes everything fertile. Adrien listened to these legends fascinated, entering into his father's childhood. Sometimes Fernand placed his hand on the boy's shoulder, just his hand, as a kind of caress. In the shoemaker's old Peugeot, which brought them home in the evening, they sang "The Brave Sailor Returns from the War" or "The Beautiful Girl of Parthenay," and then there was the pleasure of proudly displaying their catch for Clémence to admire. Worn out by the sun, Adrien fell asleep over his plate. In his bed, eyes closed, he endlessly followed the cork descending the blinding water. He tried to remember certain phrases that Fernand had said to him, but he couldn't catch the words again; he heard only the hushed voice, the warm, peaceful voice of his father, and he fell asleep happy.

The yard was empty. He put away his notebooks and pencils, cautiously climbed down the big ladder, and patted Sirène, who had heard him moving about and was waiting for him, bouncing happily. He looked for his mother. She had left the little sheds and was busy with several pots and the big cast-iron casserole, which seemed to indicate unusual preparations. He offered to help her, but she chased him off with a "keep out of the way!" which meant he was more of a nuisance than a help.

"Why don't you go over to Albert Mainson's," she said. "I really don't need you this morning. But come back before lunch so we don't keep your father waiting."

Adrien ran toward the road as he called good-bye. He couldn't have wished for a nicer offer. Albert was his favorite companion, especially when Alice was there to make things up. She always won at the game of falsehoods: "One day when it was night, I walked running in the freezing heat..." When the boys carved boats from pine bark in the form of Indian canoes that floated in the trough of the pump, she suggested that they dissolve a ball of blue soap powder to make it look like the ocean, and she made enormous waves for the canoes to sink in; or else she organized championships for spinning tops that they made from oak galls stuck with matches, slingshot competitions with old boxes set on a wall for targets, or courses for tanks made from empty spools that they slit along the edges and threaded with a rubber band twisted around a twig, so that they shot forward when they let them go. Their games were not always so peaceful. The Thursday before, Alice had led an expedition to rob magpie nests, ending triumphantly in an omelet that Albert's mother had agreed to cook. They all had eaten two mouthfuls, enjoying it thoroughly, even though it was atrocious. Alice was indispensable.

He stopped by her house, and her vacant-eyed mother said yes to the adventure, though she'd hardly heard the question. At Albert's, they called for him in vain. Finally, his big sister came out. Albert wasn't there. He'd gone with his father to sow the alfalfa.

"What should we do?" said Adrien.

"Wait, I'm thinking," said Alice.

"We could go get a little of my money from home for candy at Sonnette's."

"No," said Alice, "she left to make her rounds on Thursday, and I never have any luck with her daughter."

On the grocery store counter, a wheel mounted on a pedestal displayed ten squares marked from ten to twenty, each between two points that clicked against the spring of an old corset stay when you spun the wheel, indicating the number of candies won at the end of a turn. The pleasure lay in hearing the clicking slow down, then stop, at the fateful box, but the old shopkeeper, who was goodness itself, always corrected bad luck's shortfalls, her whole round, flat face smiling, her eyes merely cracks. She made her rounds in an old covered wagon like the ones used by pioneers in the American West, as depicted in the engravings illustrating novels by Captain Mayne Reid, or in one of those film that Monsieur Loiseau, the acrobat, showed. To signal her arrival, she rang the little bell that had given her her nickname. You could ask her for oil, or soap, dried cod, smock fabric, big pieces of wool to make cloaks, shoelaces, needles, square elastic for slingshots, and she said in a sweet, very high-pitched voice, "Wait, I'll go see if I have that," and disappeared under the cover. Sometimes, when it was late at night and she hadn't returned, her daughter went to look for her and would find the wagon stopped, her mother and the horse both asleep in the glow of the hurricane lamp hung over the harness. She especially liked children and often slipped Adrien a roll of licorice or a little box of cocoa powder as big as a thimble. A pinch under the tongue or in a glass of water was a delicious treat.

"I never get more than thirteen or fourteen with her daughter," said Alice. "Keep your money for later. Wait, maybe… What time do you have to be back?"

"For lunch."

"Then I think we have time. You know what we'll do, since it's just the two of us?"

She lowered her voice and said in a whisper, "We'll go see if what you found in the Champarnaud woods under the leaves is still there."

"We'll go together," said Adrien, a little nervous. "You'll come with me into the woods?"

"Yes, of course, since we're together."

"And even if we find it again, you won't say anything to any-one?"

"Not to anyone, since it's a secret."

"Okay!" said Adrien firmly.

They ran toward the narrow stony path that led down from the Bastière to the valley. After the last house, the hedge stopped at the entrance to the pasture. Since the wall was quite low, they saw the high plane tree at the edge of the meadow on the other side of the road and, a little farther on, Emile, the basket maker, who worked beside a fire in front of his trailer and lifted his head, hearing the stones echo or roll under their feet. They quietly followed the road to Pont-Bertrand, made a quick detour to the washing place for the pleasure of seeing the transparent water running over the long flat stones, climbed the path under the tunnel of elms, and soon freed the gate from the little barrel ring on the post that held it. Adrien pushed the gate shut behind them.

"No one saw us but Emile," said Adrien. "No one knows we're here."

Alice noticed immediately the moss house laid out under the ash tree, with its walls hardly higher than the cuckoo flowers, which had been scattered about in one corner by pecking blackbirds. They both sat down on the moss carpet, and Alice sighed deeply, as if she had finally come home.

"Is this where you learn your lessons? That big stone, is that your table?"

"Yes, to put my notebooks on. When I've had enough of playing by myself, I read my books."

"How far you can see from here!" said Alice stretching both her arms. "Over there, it's all flat, it must go to the end of the world. And maybe there's the sea after that."

"Surely," said Adrien.

For a long time he looked at Alice, carried away by so much space. Then memories came back, which seemed to preoccupy him.

"Are you always unhappy?" he asked finally.

"Yes," said Alice.

"I'm asking you that because at home I heard my father telling my mother about something he'd read in the newspaper. I looked for the paper and I read it, too. It really happened. It was a boy like me, on a farm, but bigger than me, they made him work all the time, worse than a servant, they punished him, they didn't give him enough to eat. So then, because he was hungry, he secretly ate the calves' cereal. And one day, the woman he worked for caught him with his mouth full of cereal and his hand in the sack, and to punish him, she stuck his head in the sack and she held him there so long that he suffocated to death."

"He was really dead?" asked Alice. "Dead like my papa?"

"Yes, dead, and they put the woman in prison."

"That isn't the same kind of unhappiness. But what about you?"

"Me? My father's only beaten me once."

"Beaten you hard?"

"Yes, once, really hard."

"What had you done?"

"It was a cow who got away from me while I was reading. She found some really fresh young alfalfa, and afterward she began to swell up. I was afraid she'd die. My father pierced her belly with a special little blade, the swelling very slowly went down, and then he really let me have it! And that time, my mother let him thrash me without saying anything. The next day I didn't go to school. But that doesn't mean anything; Maman and my father, I'm not their servant, it's like I'm their son."

"You go by their name."

"My father takes care of me. He takes me fishing. I eat very well, I go to school, Maman kisses me. And then I have you and Maria. I can't be unhappy."

"That story you told me, it's tragic."

"Yes. Maman said, 'Poor little one, poor little one.'"

"It's tragic," Alice repeated.

She felt fragile again, as each time this word summarized the painful lack of her father, whom absence had cut off from her. She breathed deeply, as if to fill herself once more with the immense countryside that brought her back to the soft shadow of the ash, the moss house, the little nearby woods. The object of their escapade suddenly seemed enormous to her.

"Do we have time or do we have to go back right now?"

"You're the one with the watch," said Adrien.

The expedition made him nervous, too, but not because of its length. His smock would protect his sweater this time from the thorns, which slid over it without sticking. But that man-size tool that might still be over there suddenly seemed dangerous to him, evil, almost too big, it overreached his universe. It made him confused and anxious, but he reacted bravely and got up.

"Come," he said, taking Alice's hand, "first we'll go to my hiding place."

The phrase "hiding place" made the little girl so curious that it seemed to take away all her fear. Adrien led her to the entrance where the bluebells farthest from the thicket were beginning to fade.

"First we go on hands and knees. Don't be afraid," he said, "there's nothing to poke you."

They straightened up when they got to the inner chamber surrounded by a very dense thicket with periwinkles flowering on one side, and they sat down huddled against each other on a soft, thick layer of dead leaves. There was a deep silence, only a few cries of birds above, made less lively by the calm of brooding. The rounded walls and roof of leaves gave the hiding place the look of a nest protected from all sides. Alice regarded this sanctuary with wide happy eyes gleaming with wonder.

"It's like a house," she said very quietly. "It's *your* house."

Also in a hushed voice, Adrien told her about Robinson Crusoe. He told her how he played there all alone as though he were on a desert island and showed her his supply of provisions, where the ants had eaten the little square of apple. He told her about the imaginary muskets and the oak galls that served as ammunition. He imagined what he was soon going to possess, and that reality swept aside all further ideas of play. He turned around and, now accustomed to the dark, he could distinguish at the edge of the woods the collapsing stones of the old wall, its black summit outlined against the light of the plain.

"Stay here," he murmured. "I'll call you if I need help."

He crawled, half on his knees, avoiding the treachery of a few brambles, lifting the lowest branches of the wild spindle trees, and finally reaching the pile of dead leaves in the darkest part of the hollow. Very slowly, he moved away a few of the leaves, drew his hand back quickly as it encountered the icy steel, and then screwing up his courage for what he had to do, which was serious and irreparable, he lay bare the entire gun. Still he hesitated. He could remake the leaf pile without touching anything and leave again, but now he had almost gone too far. Now he knew it really was a gun, and then there was Alice, waiting. He grabbed the weapon by the handle of the butt and pulled. It came free from its bed of leaves and shone in the light, which seemed to come from the ground itself. Crawling backward, sometimes on his knees, sometimes on his stomach, hauling his prize along in jerks, he returned to the hideout, where he sat down with a triumphant sigh.

"There it is," he said, pushing the weapon toward Alice, who moved back, stunned.

"Is it loaded?" she asked timidly.

"We'll see, I know what to do," said Adrien.

Some Sundays in winter, when the sun lit up the frost in the plowed furrows, Lortier had taken him to hunt larks with decoys. The little birds, bewitched by the glittering bits of glass set into the twirling wooden mirror on a string that Adrien, thirty meters away, kept winding and unwinding, glided as they flew about.

Lortier shot, Adrien leaped toward the ball of feathers, finally captured though it was now lifeless, which he grasped in his hands with a dazed horror and brought back in triumph. He had seen Lortier handle his gun. He seized the rifle butt firmly and pushed the latch. The bolts opened all by themselves, the barrel swung down, a cartridge was still inserted in the breech. With effort, Adrien drew it out. It must have swollen in the dampness of the woods. It was empty. A slight and surprising odor of powder filled the hideout, which, for Adrien, suddenly took on the dimensions of a fortress. He was both dumbfounded and transported by this real gun that he held on his knees. Alice had taken the cartridge and was examining it curiously.

"It's used," said Adrien. "You see the little hollow, there, on the cap. It's through there that the fire starts the powder. Lortier explained it to me."

Suddenly, it was all so obvious it stunned him; he understood everything. This was the murderer's weapon. This cartridge had killed Alice's father. But at the same time he told himself that he was holding it now, that terrible gun. He trembled. He had the feeling of victory. Alice sniffed the cardboard tube.

"It smells of death," she said.

"Yes, maybe it does," said Adrien.

"And what if he comes back to look for it?"

"Who?"

"The one who was running, the brown jacket."

"He would have come already. He wants it to stay hidden."

"I'm a little afraid."

"It's all right," said Adrien.

With his fingernail, he scraped off the small, very bright cres-
cents of rust that the leaves had left on the barrel. He closed the
empty gun, wiped it quickly with his handkerchief, opened it,
closed it again. He held it close to Alice's ear.

"Listen," he said.

He pressed on one and then the other trigger. There were two
little sharp, clear noises. Alice's thin, heart-shaped face was very
pale, her huge eyes staring fixedly at Adrien. He rested the barrel
on the little fork of wood that usually supported the childish sticks
he used as muskets. He was getting used to it. He placed the empty
cartridge near the oak galls, and a kind of fever made him nearly
exultant now, the intoxication that came from this weapon's odor
of oiled steel, its sleek and cold touch, its formidable weight, the
idea that it had murdered, but that now it was his.

"What are you going to do?" asked Alice in a very small voice.

"This afternoon, you'll watch my cows for a moment, and I'll
come here. I'll bring some rags, and I'll wrap the gun in them very
tight. No one will find it, not even that other man if he looks for it.
It's ours."

"Like the secret," said Alice.

She lowered her eyes for a long time, and then suddenly looked
into those of the boy with a gaze as shimmering as the reflections
that attracted the larks.

"Kiss me," she said out loud.

That voice, suddenly strong after all their whispering, and what
she said filled Adrien with wonder. Awkwardly, he took the little
girl in his arms, leaned her back on the leaves, and held her tightly
against himself, in a kind of heavenly joy. So close to him, her eyes

grew larger until they became a single mauve berry, and then her head of bright waving curls rested on his shoulder. He gently placed his lips on a temple where light blond tendrils fell, caressed the hair, and kissed her cheek, for a very long time. Suddenly he felt the monstrous desire to savagely undress Alice, to kiss her all over as they had formerly done in the hedge, to press her frantically against himself. But this was the flash of a forbidden desire that he held back. In his ear, he heard Alice murmuring in a very soft voice what she had already said to him once before.

"When I'm grown up, I want the two of us to be together always."

"Always," said Adrien, very softly.

A new feeling stirred in him, a solemn pride, immense, and almost painful. It implied in some confused way an unnamed duty that he only knew to be inexorable and that made him exalt. He kissed Alice, thinking triumphantly that now she was happy.

In the evening, the main gate of the Guérinière was opened wide and already Sirène had run ahead of the herd and blocked the road, but the animals knew their way home and peacefully entered the yard.

"Have they had water?" called Fernand from the barn.

"Yes, at the ford," Adrien called back to him.

"Your goats didn't act too crazy?"

"No, at the Noue, never. But Roussette got away from me again. I had to hunt for her in the poplars."

"It's her nature, that cow," said Fernand. "The stalls are ready. I'll hitch them up, you don't need to take care of that. You know your lessons?"

"All but one."

"Ah," said Fernand good-humoredly, "then you must have been playing in the fields. Go in quickly now and learn it."

Adrien had already undone his pack and put down his stick. He ran toward the house, where Clémence must have killed a rabbit; the pan was near the fire, the stove red-hot, and a blood-soaked cloth still hung from the table in the back kitchen. Hearing him, she came out of the little room that served as the dairy.

"That smells good, that tart," said Adrien.

"Dried plums," said Clémence, smiling. "And I made you a turnover for tomorrow."

"Oh! Thank you, Maman!" said Adrien happily.

That was his favorite dessert. The cooking and the tart in the middle of the week seemed to him a sign that they would be having company.

"Yes," said Clémence. "Zacharie is replacing the old planks in the hayloft, and your father asked him to have supper with us."

"I'll learn my lesson, and then I'm going to see him," cried Adrien from the stairs.

Normally, he did his schoolwork in the big room, even though his books and notebooks were kept on a little table in his bedroom. But the skylight in the loft didn't allow in much light and Clémence found the electric light too expensive. He really had been playing at the Noue. They had begun to make a dam at the outlet of the ford. Earlier, without anyone seeing him, he had returned to Champarnaud. Despite his fear in the woods alone where nothing seemed the same as it had in the morning, he had done what he had to do. The well-polished gun was now wrapped in rags, slipped under the intertwining branches of the privets and half invisible. The enormity of this secret, henceforth inseparable from Alice, gave Adrien an audacity that surprised him. In some sly way, it urged him to go beyond his usual routines and even to challenge the prohibitions. There were moments when the thought of what lay there in his hiding place oppressed him, and then that anguish was erased, blurred by a glorious pride in having vanquished all those fears to become master of this thing that even some men feared. He turned on the light, climbed up on his chair, and searched along the beam, between the two joists, for the notebook where he wrote down what seemed important to him, or simply those sentences he found beautiful. But what he reread there seemed far away from him. His morning had taken him beyond all that. To retell it would reduce it to something resembling all those days in the past. The words would sap its power. He put the notebook back in its place.

His lesson learned, he went down, whistling, into the yard where Fernand was leaving the stable with buckets full of milk. He didn't often milk his cows, and Adrien smiled with pleasure at seeing him this way, solid and strong, carrying his pails. In front of the stable, a ladder had been raised to the open shutters of the hayloft, and someone was hammering above. He climbed up and first made out a bundle of wide strips of floorboard, their size explaining why they had been brought up through the outside window. Then he saw Zacharie, who was hard at work replacing the boards along the openings through which hay was made to fall directly into the hayracks below.

"Aha! There's my apprentice!" said the old carpenter cheerfully. "Exactly what I need, a hand to hold my board. Be careful not to fall down in front of your cows' noses. Wedge your foot in there and push the lath. Very good!"

The boards were grooved. Once fit together and well tightened with a mallet, he nailed them diagonally, then hammered the tips in such a way that they disappeared into the wood. The strong odor of freshly planed pine contrasted sharply with the more diffuse scent of hay. When the hammer stopped, you could hear the clinking of the cows' collars as they moved about below, and farther away the strange bleating of a goat who perhaps had caught its foot in its chain and was complaining.

"It's too dark in this corner," said Zacharie at last, "I can't see more than half my troubles anymore. I'll finish that tomorrow morning. My hammer will be waking you up, my boy."

Adrien went down the inside ladder. Behind him, the goat was still bleating. It must be the mother. As soon as his foot touched the ground, he looked her in the eyes and felt sudden alarm. She was bleating as she searched with her nose the straw where the little kid goat ought to have been lying. Adrien bounded into the yard. His father was coming out of the cellar, closing the door with one hand, holding the bottles of wine for dinner in the other. Adrien ran, seized by what he had already guessed and violently rejected. He rushed toward his father, his fists out, his voice tight.

"My little goat?" he cried. "My little goat?"

"Ah!" said Fernand very gently, "so you know. We thought so. Your mother did say that this would be hard for you, but there was no way around it. Your little goat, we'll be eating a bit of it tonight."

"You've killed it?"

"I'm afraid so. You see?" said Fernand, pointing to the manure pile, its black top, strewn with dirty straw, rising higher than the wall separating it from the little pond where ducks were still swimming.

This was so terrible that Adrien pressed his two fists against his mouth without crying out, his face clenched in mute sobs. On the manure pile, the baby goat's head looked up to the sky, elongated by the limp remains of its skin, from which dangled its little split hooves.

A furious despair suddenly seized him, and he threw himself at his father, hammering him with his fists, crying, "No! No!" making it necessary for Fernand to step back in order not to be knocked over. Disconcerted by this violence, Fernand held him back with his free hand and said in what he hoped was a soothing tone, "Whoa, Adrien, come on now! Come on now, Adrien, stop!" The boy abruptly stopped hitting, crying silently. Fernand put down his bottles, sat down on the little wall of the steps, and took Adrien by the hand.

"Sit down here, my little fellow," he said, patting his knee. "I have to explain something to you. Are you listening carefully to me?"

Adrien nodded through his tears.

"That baby goat, we could have let it get big, but we've got six goats. That's plenty for making cheese and your mother has a hard time milking them all, you understand? So we raised it like the geese and the rabbits: for food, like the pig this winter. Did you cry when we killed the pig? No? Maybe you could have cried for him, even if you didn't love him."

"You don't have to kill what I love," said Adrien, hiccuping. "The pig I don't mind."

"Listen carefully. With a farm like ours, first of all, there're the fields, then there're the animals. For us, for farmers, it's all one harvest. You harvest in the fields, and you harvest in the stables, in the henhouses, in the pigpens."

He continued, in clumsy words but with great patience, to lay out the hard facts that governed them: you cultivated the fields and you raised animals to eat. Everything went hand in hand, breeding and sowing, fattening and fertilizing, slaughtering and harvesting. And the slaughter and harvest were holidays because they signified the fruits of long labor, because meat and bread were nourishing. And likewise, you gathered what grew or lived in the wild, baskets full of mushrooms, cherries, or greens from the fields, nets filled with fish, game bags stuffed with beautiful hare. Those animals you didn't raise to kill, you required to be useful—cows for their milk, goats for pulling carts, dogs and cats for protecting and hunting. The others were condemned from the time they were born. It was better to be born a boy than a baby goat.

"You didn't hurt him too much?" asked Adrien, who was trying to stifle his sobs.

"Of course not! That, I swear to you. Off you go! Wipe your tears and then take these two bottles into the house."

Adrien blew his nose and left. When he'd gone a few steps, Fernand said sadly, raising his voice, "You're going to have to harden your heart, my boy!"

Adrien didn't turn around, didn't look back at the manure pile or the stable, where Zacharie, who had to put his tools away, was now calmly climbing down from the hayloft. He entered the house and put the two bottles on the table. Clémence, who had put her pan on the fire, saw his face, quickly wiped her hands on her apron, and hugged Adrien close, kissing him on the forehead.

"It really had to happen," she said softly. "You'll see, you'll forget him. Maybe the next time, we can keep one."

Dinner was lively, nevertheless, thanks to Zacharie. His presence compelled Adrien to keep his despair in check, and even if he hardly ate, he listened. Fernand was having one of his good days, his mind quick and light. His morning seemed to have cleansed and rejuvenated him; as always when he worked his fields, he felt his solid peasant dignity restored. And with the wild burning that wine alone could placate lying dormant, he forgot it was lurking deep within him. He drank only to quench his thirst and refilled his guest's glass more often than his own. At these times, he rediscovered the curiosity that used to make him take an interest in everything, especially what went beyond his own world to that elsewhere he knew only through the papers. He had skillfully gotten Zacharie onto the subject of his Tour de France, and the old carpenter told how he had first worked in Tours and in the navy workshops in Nantes, where, still quite young, he had learned the basics of the art of sketching, and then in Bordeaux, where his master had taught him the art of design, of working warped, curved, or sloped pieces, and of designing a good gyron for stairs, pulpit panels for churches, or the arch of a cornice. He described the beauty of rivers and bridges, cathedrals, architectural works for which he still knew the five orders. He recalled the way of life of the people in these countries, what they cultivated in the rural areas, the unknown trees that he had discovered as he headed south: olive, lotus trees, and even lemon. In Narbonne, he had touched the enormous snail shell used as a basin for holy water in the cathedral. He had gone to Saint-Gilles-du-Gard, where so many journeyman stonecutters had engraved their names on the walls of the mysterious stairwell, where still no one really knew how the stones for it could have been cut and assembled. His tour had ended at Angoulême in the cattle trucks that carried him to the front, but even though this subject interested Fernand very much, Zacharie refused to talk about the First World War.

Silent, Clémence served her table, attentive to everyone. When the meat came out—which she had sautéed in the frying pan with fresh garlic—without a word, she placed before Adrien a pâté that he loved, and that he thanked her for with his look but hardly touched. He listened without hearing, now and then catching bits of what the two men were saying. Instinctively, he located on the French map the cities Zacharie named, but more often, his grief closed in on him, confused and violent. He glimpsed death there, what had touched Alice. The events of the morning seemed to him very old and almost unreal. They retreated into a closed past where the memory of the gun disturbed him. He would have preferred that the gun had disappeared from his life, taking with it the dull anxiety that was all that was left of what the weapon had awakened.

When he had eaten his share of the tart, Clémence reminded him how late it was and that it was time to go to bed. He nodded to Zacharie and said good night to his father, who didn't just put his hand on his shoulder as usual but drew him close and kissed him.

"I'll be up shortly to tuck you in," said Clémence cheerfully as he closed the door behind him.

Adrien walked along the dark corridor. Even though he hadn't shown it, his father's long explanations and his mother's gentle attempts to lighten his grief hadn't diminished his resentment. Maybe they wanted to be forgiven, but they were guilty. He felt alone with his sorrow, dispossessed of the soft little coat that he had loved to caress, decidedly alone and vaguely realizing that he would always be so. He didn't go upstairs right away but noiselessly opened the front door and slipped into the yard.

It was late when Zacharie took his leave. While Clémence cleared the table and put the food away in the kitchen larder, Fernand made a tour of the stables, treated his horse to a little barley, and put a handful of salt in the manger of the old goat, who had stopped bleating. He was content. The moon meant good weather, the clover would dry without risk, he had had a good talk with his son. He had only half a glass of wine before going to bed, and that restraint added to the feeling that his day had been complete.

As soon as everything was put away, Clémence washed her hands and went up to kiss Adrien good night. There was a beam of light under the door, which she opened halfway. Adrien was asleep. The head of the little goat lay next to him on its ear, sticking out of a sack in which he had carefully rolled up the bloody hide, and which he held close to him with both arms. His hand still caressed the white spot, in the familiar hollow between the two little bumps that could never become horns now. Bordered by long lashes, the eyes in that head were misty green, the gray tongue sticking out between clenched teeth and seeming to lick his companion's forehead.

Clémence smiled sadly, turned off the light, walked on tiptoes down to the kitchen, sat down on a chair, her hand resting on the oilcloth on the table, worn out, a knot of bottomless pain in her throat. She hadn't been able to console the little one. There were still dishes to do, goats to milk. The night had begun.

X

zacharie

ZACHARIE WASN'T SLEEPING. From his bed, oriented in the way Angèle had liked it in days gone by, he followed the slow course of the full May moon through the open window, its light giving the same secret solidity to all forms. Even though he was old, and despite all the years, his memory brought Angèle back to this room where she thought the moon with its milky liqueur would help her have children. Later, when her belly had slowly followed the star's great course, she had thanked God and the moon for it, although neither she nor Zacharie, who were wrapped up in the happiness of waiting, ever once dreamed that this would be her undoing. She had died in childbirth, along with the infant. Though he only realized the full extent of the damage later, with everything that came to a stop there, the destruction of his faith—already broken by the war—was complete. But the moon had retained for him a glow in which was reflected the sweetness of his love for his wife. He saw her there again, leaning on her elbows at the window in her long nightgown, faded white so it looked lunar itself. He remembered how before going to sleep, his sister used to recite, "Moon, my beautiful silver mirror, show me in my sleep who my suitor will be." She told how many times she had seen, always outlined in black, the face of the boy she had later married, who had died in the first months of the war. His grandmother was sure that the silhouette drawn upon the moon was Job's, forever carrying his bundle of sticks, whom you had to ask, after your prayers, for protection from raging dogs, snakebites, and the temptation of Satan. Zacharie, his wide-awake eyes on that great pale face passing his window, saw a kind of sad smile there instead.

His Tour de France and the war had taught him not to become attached to either places or things. He only held on to his tools and his books, and loved to travel. He had worked in one workshop after another, from Tours to Saintes, and he remembered this period as a kind of childhood, wandering and carefree. He had earned his guild name, his stick, and his colors in La Rochelle, his earring in Nantes, and he had become a full guild member in Angoulême. At Surgères, he had worked for the master Vernoux, who was Angèle's father. But Angèle's brother had his workbench in the workshop, so one day he would be the master, and Angèle and Zacharie had no hope of a future there. After the wedding, they had left Surgères for Niort, and then his father had offered to share the little village carpentry shop with him. There, he had an electric planer installed immediately, and the business, which he called his practice, doubled in two years. Zacharie knew how to draw any form and cut wood perfectly. He carved and jigsawed the fronts and bottom crosspieces of armoires, did the interiors of shops in Niort, but also put together, all by himself, a cart to which Barberade, the cartwright, added wheels. After Angèle's death, he felt like a glove without a hand, unable to grasp on to anything. Everything that supported him had collapsed. He worked himself to death, trained several apprentices, and passed on his knowledge, as his Devoir order wished, to fellow guild members, drawn to him by the reputation of his great skill. He never refused to take them on. He knew that he was a link in a chain it was his responsibility not to break. One day in the frame of a chest of drawers he was restoring, he found a very old piece of paper all folded up, on which he read, "Greetings to the carpenter who takes apart this chest of drawers and finds this paper. Let him have a mass said for my soul's repose, Charles Vigneron, Bressuirais La Ténacité." Zacharie was only familiar with Protestant religion, but he went to find the parish priest, and Charles Vigneron had his mass, greetings, and brotherhood, by God!

As old age set in, he had retired first one of the three workbenches in the workshop, and then the second one. Now his alone served for the bit of work the village needed done. He had once again become a small-time carpenter as his father had been, and only his students remembered Poitevin Noble Coeur, master *menuisier du Devoir,* who now needed glasses to draw straight. He told himself that his trade and his life were so well blended that they had married the same curve. During the Second World War, his solitude had at least allowed him to hide those great redheaded flyers and the young one with his radio, who was later killed in combat. Now, when he was alone and unoccupied, his naturally cheerful and sociable character often turned melancholy. Angèle's face—as youthful as it appeared in their photograph, despite the passing years—or rather the vague sadness of her absence, came back painfully to haunt the old man he had become. There she was, elbows on the windowsill, streaming with the white sap of the full moon.

"Let me tell you all about this, my little Angèle," Zacharie began his monologue. "That Germain Brunet, to say hello to him or a word or two when you go to get your hair cut at Cécile's, all right. But I can't say anyone really got along with him. His innocent-child manner and his smiles, he offers you everything with all his heart, it's a bit too much, so in the end you don't trust him. And always praising himself to the skies, everything he does is going to turn out great. And what does he do? First of all he hollows out and lines two big pools in a field that his father-in-law had below Font-maillol. It seems that the water in these pools is so cold the trout are going to multiply ten times in the wink of an eye. But since that water comes right out of the earth, it doesn't provide anything to eat, so every day he has to feed the fish on powdered shrimp. And since herons come, too, he has to fight off the herons and put up a fence on account of thieves. Finally, the whole thing goes to ruin, the sides of the pools collapse, the walls are good for eels, the shel-ter for the sacks and nets that fatten up and catch those famous trout serves as a hideout for thrush hunters in the poplars. After-ward, he wants a chicken yard for roosters, little fighter cocks with red, bronze, bluish tails.

"One Sunday morning when there were three or four of us waiting there for Cécile to shave us, he showed us that, and I have to say, he wasn't bad at it. He ties up one or two feathers by wrap-ping them around a fishhook held tight in a little vise. With scissors he cuts off what's too long, and it's an imitation fly, but you'd swear it was an ephemera, a dragonfly, a mayfly. These he sold for a little while in the Saint-Maixent and Niort tackle shops, and then you didn't hear any more about them. Maybe the cocks molted, or the flies didn't feed their man. So after that, he turns to raising ponies, but instead of preparing the old trout meadow with its stream for them, he fences in a bare field in the Minées, without a single leaf for shade, where he installs half an old cask, because he's got to carry in water. The four ponies and donkey fenced in there soon strip the grass clean, and he has to put up a hayrack and give them hay. But animals, too, are hard on each other. The ponies never let the donkey get his hay. One of them was always in front of the rack to chase him away. The poor donkey ended up getting so weak that he spent all his time lying down right in the hot sun. He only got up when he saw Maria, who took pity on him and gave him old carrots or handfuls of grass or bran through the fence, and he'd eat them from her hand. Germain really made fun of all that. Maria ended up coming nearly every day. She said, 'Look at him, that poor donkey, the poor thing, with his sad eyes and long lashes!'

"Who knows why Germain left for eight days without saying where he put the keys to the padlocks on the gate. Cécile claimed that he'd gone to the wedding of one of his nephews, but the gossip was about prison, without anyone really knowing anything exactly. And it's true that you learn not to leave anything lying around when Germain comes by, because he has a reputation for having a quick hand when it comes to pocketing this or that. Poor Simon had told me that the Hunting Association was keeping an eye on him ever since he'd been caught one night with a long net extended all the way along to the end of a field of Jerusalem artichokes. He came down through the field very quietly, rounding up a flock of partridges who ran in front of him before going headfirst into the net. He always took off in the middle of summer, leaving his meadow, the cask dry, his animals dying of thirst, and Cécile, who didn't care. Maria no longer knew what to do. She went to find Mainson, who has a tank mounted on an old cart frame for carrying water when he tends his vineyard. Between them, they hooked up the end of a gutter running from the fence to the cask and they filled it. So the ponies, who drank nonstop, were saved, but they wouldn't let the donkey, who could hardly get to his feet, come close. Finally, the donkey lay down and died. From then on, I said to myself that this Germain had a heart of stone."

Zacharie shifted to the side of the bed to follow the moon as it slid along. He had seen evil people almost everywhere, insensitive, tightfisted masters, deceitful and treacherous workers, aggressive guild members and even thieves who had to be expelled from the brotherhood by breaking their sticks and burning their colors. In the village, when he was younger, there was Rabistoque, who scared people with that other disciple who followed him like a dog. He was called l'Hirondelle, because he climbed up high into the poplars to prune them. Both of them sly weasels asking for their handout from Méhus de Cherves come Saturday, but you wouldn't want to meet either of them in some dark corner of the woods at night. When his sister did her dressmaking apprenticeship with that horrible old woman, who cut her with little jabs of her needle for the tiniest fault, Rabistoque had waited for her two or three times in the valley she had to cross coming home. He followed her in a threatening way. Zacharie had taken his grandfather's wolf pike, a solid staff with a little two-pointed steel fork at the end, and he had gone to wait for Louise, too. He had it out with Rabistoque, who never had to be warned again. But neither Rabistoque nor l'Hirondelle would have ever killed anyone. That was for clumsy and drunk bandits, brutish marauders.

This unbelievable business, so terrible that the pale disc smiled down on it with pity, was first suspected by the fish seller. The fish seller knows the whole village, the chance result of his rounds, reads words and gestures, listens to the stories, peddles the news, or keeps disclosed secrets to reveal them when he wishes, like a weapon. It was afternoon, maybe half an hour after the supposed hour of the double crime. He arrived at the crossroads, at the top of the stone path that descends sharply to the lower bridge. He saw a man climb this path running and then, when he noticed the car, turn off suddenly toward the footpaths leading to the back of the village. He did not see him long enough to recognize him, but he was sure that the man's jacket was brown. It seemed to him that it was a hunting jacket with the game pocket in back stretched tight and heavy. The time of day, and especially the fact that the man was running as he climbed a slope that ordinarily made you out of breath, interested the police very much. Here was someone who was in a hurry to return, who changed routes not to be seen, who cut across toward the higher trails, through uncultivated fields and thickets where he wouldn't pass anyone. If this person were the murderer, it had to be someone from here.

It's impossible to question all the men in a village, two or three of whom were in the fields at the time indicated by the fish seller, often alone, with unverifiable alibis. On the other hand, you can imagine checking the weapons, which had remained hidden during the war to escape being confiscated, and which had only just begun to reappear. The list of hunting licenses gave the names of those who owned guns, and the police conducted a long inquiry, not overlooking the houses of widows and old people indicated by the mayor, where there could still be an old weapon. This was the case with Maria, where Abraham's gun was still in the clock, all clean on the outside, though the barrels were eaten away by rust. The inquiry revealed that nearly all the hunters had cleaned weapons, with grease that had hardened many months ago. The traces of powder left by the negligent were analyzed. None had been fired recently. The guns differed little. Many of them were Robuste de la Manufacture. There were three dog-hunting rifles and two Lefacheux with pin cartridges, one at Amédée Gornard's, who, at eighty, still got his two partridges with each double shot, the other at Germain Brunet's. The inspections revealed nothing.

One of the police had the idea of checking the ammunition, which nearly everyone made at home. Each person got out his supply of shot, caps, cartridge cases, wads, cartons, or his bought, ready-made cartridges. Nobody had yet begun to make any cartridges, and there were many empty cases, often put away neatly with the boxes of new caps. Old Amédée Gornard had about fifty pin cartridges, Germain Brunet had three of them. That wasn't right.

"Yes, of course that's right!" Germain said. "You don't really think I hunt with this old blunderbuss, do you? How would you like me to show you my Robuste. I took it to be checked over."

"Yes, that's true," said Cécile, astonished, "it's been a little while since I've seen it in its place, that gun of yours."

"Look, here are the cartridges, a good forty of them, and the caps. My goodness! I showed you my grandfather's gun, since you wanted to see a gun. I'll bring you my Robuste as soon as it comes back. It'll be as good as new."

"And where did you take it to have it checked over, this Robuste?"

"Where? Where did I take it? Well, to Sabiron in Niort, of course."

"And you wouldn't have some kind of paper, a proof of deposit?"

"Me? From Sabiron? Where I've been going at least fifteen years? So maybe you don't believe me, by chance?"

"Yes, of course, my dear sir, I believe you."

"Because, if you wish, I can go get it right now and show it to you, this gun."

"No! No! It's at Sabiron's, of course. Of course we believe you, dear Monsieur Brunet. But if it's not too much trouble, could we see your hunting jacket?"

"My jacket? But I don't even know where my jacket is!"

"Your brown jacket?" said Cécile. "I'm the one who washed it, but it hasn't been ironed yet."

"It doesn't matter, Madame Brunet, it's not important, just a detail, just asking. Thank you very much."

The police had no sooner left than the next day Germain told Cécile he had to go see his uncle in Parthenay, that he hadn't had any news for a while, and that he had to go see about the inheritance. He put on his suit, packed his bag, got the old Citroën he'd bought to astonish everyone out of the barn, threw his bag in the back, and turned around. There was a policeman standing in front of the hood.

"And where are you going like that, my dear sir? To Sabiron's?"

"I move around as I wish. It's a free country now, isn't it?"

"That," said the police, whose manner all of a sudden changed, "is an entirely different matter. So, you dog, you want to vanish into thin air and have us come back three days later to find nothing? Your name's written all over your crime! You're the only one who's lost your gun, which your gunsmith's never seen. And I guarantee you that you are going to tell us where you've hidden it."

And he put on the handcuffs.

In the village, the police are not liked, nor their law, which nevertheless must be followed, nor this curiosity regarding weapons and ammunition, which makes everyone suspect. When it's learned that they've taken in Germain, it's like lightning's struck. First, everyone's suspicious: it's not possible, why would he do that? But rumor has it that he has confessed. Because Germain broke down in front of Cécile, who was screaming at him and trying to strike him, which the police let her do, until Cécile exploded into sobs and let herself be taken away to her neighbor's house. Germain told everything. From time to time, he went down into the valley by the little Bastière path to climb up by the Outremont, which the association had made a hunting reserve. There, he made his tour like someone out for a walk but kept his eyes open. Some days he didn't see anything. But when he spotted a hedge where a cock pheasant flew out, or located a hare's shelter, he would return home quickly to set out again with his usual supplies: the gun hidden away, the butt in his game pocket, the barrel slipped between his shoulder blades or into a pant leg, unseen and unsuspected at lunchtime when the fields were empty.

This unlucky day, he's walking along as if he's looking for morels, but he's late. He follows along the big hedge separating the stubble fields from the plain, in the middle of the clumps of broom, out of the wind, and suddenly he sees an enormous hare hiding there, partly covered by the wild oats, its ears lying down on its back. He almost steps on it. He continues on as if it were nothing, hurries down to the stream, crosses, and climbs back up, without meeting anyone, to the stone path that takes him almost right to his garden, behind his house. Cécile isn't there, but she certainly knows that he's in the habit of poaching, though she closes her eyes to it. It must be said that sometimes it's nice in terms of the menu. To sneak out, he waits for that hour after the whole village has left for the fields and before the herds come home. He has heard Jeandet, who's pounding stakes with a sledgehammer to reinforce the bank, and those resounding strikes suit him, since his own shots will be less noticeable. Besides, the place he's returning to now, he hasn't seen anyone working, no farming, no signs of labor.

He isn't looking very well, because when he shoots that hare, which he drains of its urine and is still holding by the feet, coming out of the hedge he runs into Simon Varadier and his hired hand, and they've heard him. He lets the hare drop, but he's still holding the gun, and it's too late.

"So it's you again!" says Simon, who is not at all pleasant about it. "And in the reserve! And right in the middle of May, when the litters are just being born! You come here to slap us in the face with hares the association had brought in from Hungary to repopulate, but this time, you bastard, you aren't going to get away with it, there are two witness for what you've done, they can't take away your permit, because you don't have one, but they can take away your gun and you'll be knocked flat by the fine, and I'm the one who you..."

He wasn't able to finish. With a terrible blast, Germain shot his second cartridge, his gun at his hip. Simon no longer had a neck, his chest gurgled from everywhere, and the other one, Fréchaud, instead of saving himself, rushes over to hold him up. Now it's all or nothing. Germain opens his gun, puts the two empty cartridges in his pocket, slips in another one, and shoulders it, aiming at Fréchaud, who has suddenly understood and runs. The shot rips his back. He falls on his stomach, has two or three convulsions, and it's over. He doesn't move again.

"Now it's a matter of not dawdling," Germain says to himself, shoving the hare in his game pocket. The herds are already in the Noue. He has to go the long way around, but first of all, he has to get rid of this gun. That's the most important thing: no one must see him with this gun. He runs, he hides it in the leaves in the first little woods he comes to on the edge of Champarnaud. Now he runs as fast as he can to get as far away as possible. He climbs back up the stone-lined shortcut from the lower bridge, sees the fish seller's truck, cuts over, returns home from the back, and, as soon as he catches his breath, pretends that he's just coming from the garden to Marie Piqueraud, who's having Cécile do her child's hair.

"Good!" says the policeman. "You've killed two men for a hare. We'll write all that down, and you'll sign it. But first, you are going to lead us to this gun, because it's the main piece of evidence for the trial."

"There's no point," says Germain.

"What do you mean, no point?"

"I tried to go find it when you wanted to see the guns. It's not there anymore."

"How can it not be there anymore?"

"The leaves had been moved, and someone took it. I looked all around. There's nothing there anymore. I don't have a gun anymore, it's been stolen."

"So that's one more matter!" says the policeman. "You wouldn't be telling me a story now?"

"We'll go there if you want to."

"Of course we'll go there!"

It was then that they left the house. A few people had gathered, having seen the police van. Lebraut stood apart, with his white shirt and his straw hat, proud as a vigilante. You could still hear Cécile's cries at the neighbor's. It became very quiet, as if Germain, with his hands bound, caused some fear. At the same time, this was someone from the village. To see him with those handcuffs was troubling. It was unbelievable. He didn't say a word. He didn't look at anyone. They went to Champarnaud and there they searched all the edges of the woods without finding anything. At that time of day, the light fell into the hollow pointed out by Germain. Someone must have seen the barrel shining among the leaves, wondered what was gleaming there, and taken the gun.

"Well!" said the policeman. "I really want to believe you, Brunet. We'll come back here later. Your Robuste is going to turn up again.

For the moment, to headquarters for the papers, and then to Niort to see the judge, and prison. And I can tell you that you aren't going to be out soon. You're head's at stake, my man."

Germain suddenly had the contrite air of a child caught in the wrong. He doesn't consider what he did. He doesn't know that it's a man's life. He only thinks of his own and has never imagined his death. For him, those shots, those bodies giving way, that's already far off, that's finished. What he regrets is being caught.

"And do I have to pay the fine for the hare, too?" he asked.

Zacharie's eyes were wide open. This story made him sick. He thought of the long, hard efforts living took, adding to life took. He thought of the hard existence of his grandfather, of the short summer nights that ended when the reapers arrived for work. At sunrise, you'd already be so tired, you'd lay down for a minute, your jacket rolled up under the small of your back to straighten it. When his grandfather began working at sixteen to feed his mother, old Poublanc had taken him into the meadow, behind the house, and had handed him a scythe, and then got down on all fours to see how close to the ground he had reaped. At eighteen, he was in charge of three workers, with the right to cut the bread like the master, as well paid as the cabbage cutter who on winter mornings was let into a field of fodder cabbage stiff with ice, with his gaitered clogs and his dog-skin knickers, who, along with his cut cabbages, was picked up again in the cart, frozen stiff himself now, too, his hands bloody from chilblains—this one had the right to put all the wood he wanted on the fire. You even worked into the evening, shelling corn on the square edge of an old frying pan handle, shelling nuts, twisting hemp for ropes, braiding straw and vines, or covering chestnut baskets with wicker. Whoever hadn't finished his basket by Mardi Gras found it full of thorns and nettles. Sometimes the old man who wove linen to make sheets on the big loom set up in the stable for the winter came to warm himself by the fire. Once your waffles were eaten, you returned together to the distant farms, huddled around the lanterns, often followed by the glimmering sparks of wolves' eyes. At Mardi Gras, the evenings ended. Boys arrived at the houses in a hullabaloo. Disguised, they were allowed to kiss young and old and eat crêpes until one of them was recognized. And because Poublanc was Catholic, six weeks of Lent followed, the height of the sowing season, in which you were fed firm cabbages, turnips, and potatoes. You danced as well, boys and girls, workers and servants, to the sound of a Jew's harp the blacksmith had made, which someone or other set singing, or with the fiddler at weddings, the only music you heard. His grandfather's stories seemed as far away to him as the scenes from the Bible read out loud by his mother when he was small, a hard time, a religious time, long past, with a pure simplicity, a great nobility. A life that had taken so long to fashion had no right to be shattered by a gunshot.

For four years, men had died under gunfire and shell fire beside him, and by some miracle, he had remained alive. These were deaths rendered ordinary by the war. You ended up thinking only of yourself. And of course, you had to kill, too. Existence was narrow and black, but you hung on, you lived in a madness that God should never have allowed, where those he punished with death weren't guilty. Perhaps he had lost interest in the living as well as the dead. But the dead were so numerous that in the end they created a kind of logic of terror, in which the illogical position was to live. The war ended, death and its buzzing swarm of wasps settled down and took up their usual course once more, according to which the old ones like him, Zacharie, waited peacefully to be carried off. Deaths such as Simon's and Fréchaud's were unjustifiable, and what Germain Brunet had done couldn't be forgiven.

Perhaps the worst part was that while Simon was being buried, Brunet had wanted to watch Alice eat that hare, as if his victim's daughter were, at the same time, eating his sin, as if he were using Alice's innocent Eucharist to obliterate the cause of his crime, to absolve himself. When Zacharie imagined that shameful invitation, which Cécile had denounced so loudly in the midst of the other evil deeds, in the grim commotion of the village, he had said to himself that the most unfortunate one of all was the one no one thought about, whose pain sharpened at knowing that her husband's murderer had a name and a face, that he had run into her and talked with her often, that he had invited her daughter to lunch. He had wanted to go see her so that she wouldn't be alone that day, and as a pretext for his visit, he brought Alice a little treasure box that he had carved long ago for Angèle when he was still in Surgères. It was a beautiful wooden shoe out of walnut, its curved end joined to a delicate figure of an angel carved in dark relief in the wood on top, and it could only be opened if you knew how to work the mechanism. When the first of the two lids lifted, the engraved initials A.V. appeared, which were also Alice's initials.

Léa's eyes were red. She had him sit down and she poured him a glass of brandy while he explained to the little one how to make the secret of the shoe work. The box made Alice so happy that Léa seemed soothed by it. They had chatted over this and that, but when her daughter had left the room with her treasure and Zacharie had gotten up to leave, Léa had suddenly buried her head in the old carpenter's shoulder, shuddering in tearless sobs. Gently holding her close, Zacharie told himself that it was always the same irreparable suffering, loving those who are no longer. She had pulled herself together when Alice returned with a piece of cloth she untied to let three lead pellets slip into the shoe, over which she closed the secret lid.

The moon had now left the window, carrying with it Angèle's ghost, but Angèle was still there, sweet and painful. "What is there left for me to tell you, my beauty?" Zacharie said to himself. "Maybe to tell you that I've changed seasons. Now it's winter that pleases me." He loved those long nights, the rain and the wind that, for centuries and centuries, drew the winter wheat out of the ground and slowly made the oaks grow, his own story, which had crossed stubbornly through the violence of men, the winter of his own life, the time that had fled. He smiled to himself, imagining that sometime much later, Alice, finding the little walnut shoe again in some drawer, would bring him back to life in thinking of him, because for a long time, things retain the memory of their dead.

adrien

THE DAM WAS NEARLY FINISHED. The day before, downstream from the ford and beginning from each bank, the children had put up two little diagonal dikes of stone and sand that forced the stream to narrow. Reaching the bottleneck between them, the suddenly swollen current took on a frothing speed for several meters, splitting into two eddies swirling peacefully over its threshold. While Edmond secured the last stones, all of them, their feet frozen, waded happily toward the shore where Albert was building mill wheels. In the slits he had made through a very straight piece of a branch serving as an axle, he slipped two other pieces split into small boards to form the four blades of a cross. This axle only had to be balanced on two forks stuck into the sand so that the ends of the blades would be pushed by the current, and the mill wheel turned all the faster since this current was stronger now. They set up four of them in a line, and Albert, shaking branches, leaves, and wood shavings from his smock, came around to inspect them. The mills turned with surprising speed, and for a moment everyone watched them in silence. Then the game became more complicated by bits of wood cut into canoes that Rosa or Alice released from the ford, which idled for a moment, and then suddenly took on inordinate speed for their size and were imperiled by the dangerous mill paddles. Or the girls released little moss rafts on which they boarded ants by means of grass blades. These navigations ended calmly in a very still cove, near the reeds, where the water barely reached the knees, in such a way that you could retrieve the skiffs and release them again upstream. But it was the mills' rapid rotation, regular and infinite, that captivated Adrien. He told himself that this whirling would continue when there was no one there anymore to watch it, that it would go on all night, and if no accident befell it, for days, for years, as long as the water ran, until the end of time, until the wooden axles and forks were reduced to rubble by so much wear. For him, this was the image of the beginning of an eternity in which his thoughts wandered, powerless and happy.

When they'd arrived at the Noue, he had dragged Alice hurriedly into the refuge in the hedge to tell her how his little goat had died. She also needed to talk to him. She was excited and talkative, tormented by the unsuspected importance that their secrets had suddenly taken on. First, she triumphantly took Zacharie's finely carved little shoe out of her bag. She hastened to show him the mechanism as though to prove to him that nothing between them could remain hidden. For her, Germain's arrest hadn't changed anything. She felt no fear retrospectively, rather a kind of indignation. The police had said that the swine would have his head cut off, and this verdict pleased her as if it had already been carried out. But the three incriminating lead pellets, now locked away inside the wooden shoe, no longer had any value as proof, since Germain had confessed everything. This wasn't true for the gun.

"They can keep looking," said Adrien. "They'll never find it where it is now, unless I tell. But if I tell, they might want to arrest me, because I've stolen it."

"They might want to especially because if you had told before, they would have arrested Germain right away. You suspected, didn't you, that this was the gun that killed Papa?"

"No, I... Yes, listen, I really thought that it was. I'm keeping it. If I tell, we don't have a secret anymore."

"Yes we do, the hideout."

"That's not enough. This gun is an enormous secret."

That was exactly what Adrien found so heavy. What he had hidden from everyone was serious. What the gun had done or could do was serious. The thought that this weapon was there—unlike what Alice felt, who considered the idea of it, more than the object—weighed upon him like a vague pain, which he couldn't locate, which he still found intact when they talked about it. At the same time, it gave him the strength of a man, the unknown sensation of a maturity through which he could vaguely make out another world, the end of childhood. He steeled himself to say, "I'm keeping it."

Adrien thought about the mills. Everyone continued playing around him, except Albert, who was tapping a piece of alder with his knife handle to loosen the bark from it and make a whistle. The dogs themselves forgot their watch, playing in the meadow, chasing each other in big circles that suddenly reversed direction, and then just as suddenly lying down, tongues hanging out, breathing loudly, or stretching their muzzles between their feet before jumping up again. The animals were calm. The goats at the foot of the stubble field wall had found a clump of brambles and were greedily devouring the young shoots. The cows carried the associations of the stables into the meadow, and each herd grazed in a group without mixing much with the others. It was enough for one of the cowherds to leave the game from time to time to make sure that everything was in order. Since the shipwrecked moss rafts and skiffs absorbed them entirely, those children who got out of the icy water for a moment to warm up their feet joined Albert and remained seated on the bank to watch the successful navigations, the sudden accelerations, and the calamities. First to leave the game, Rosa came back over the meadow, cried out that she couldn't see the goats anymore, and everyone went back up with her. Only Alice's three goats still surrounded the bramble bush there; the others had disappeared.

"They're behind the hedge, or they're just beyond the poplars," said Edmond, "at the barbed-wire fence where there's another clump of brambles. Albert, will you come with me?"

"Let's all go!" cried Alice happily.

"Look, there they are!" said Albert. "Your dog is bringing them back. Whoa! What a race! Look at that! Your dog, too, Adrien."

Led by an old head nanny goat, the tight herd swerved sharply according to the positions of the dogs, forming a moving black stain at the bottom of the poplars, all the extended heads drawing it out diagonally.

"Whistle for them, Edmond, whistle for your dogs, the goats are going to get killed!"

Adrien called Sirène, who returned at a gallop, all proud. Titan, Edmond's dog, needed coaxing. Freed from the dogs, the goats came back into the Noue at a dignified trot. Everything seemed to be in order. It was Alice who noticed that Roussette, Adrien's wayward cow, was no longer there.

"Where could that cow have gone again?" said Adrien, who quickly put his shoes back on. "She drives me crazy!"

"We didn't watch carefully enough," said Rosa.

"She's certainly not in the poplars," said Albert, "or the dogs would have brought her back. Unless she took the path below the stubble fields."

"Think about it," said Adrien, "it's all closed off that way. More likely she crossed the hedge."

"I'll go with you," said Edmond.

"We should have checked more often," said Rosa.

They disappeared behind the hedge. Settling down, Albert and the two girls drew books and notebooks from their schoolbags and began to recite their lessons. Then Rosa, who had washerwoman fingers from the game with the mills, took from her bag the dishtowels her mother had given her to hem and began to sew. The afternoon wore on.

"They're late," said Alice.

"Roussette has never gone that far," said Albert, who had gotten his knife out again and was carving his stick.

Soon Edmond appeared, alone.

"We can't find her," he said. "We went as far as the Charconnier road. You have to come help us."

"Go ahead," said Rosa, "I'll stay here and watch the others, don't worry."

All three took off again behind the hedge. Adrien was waiting for them, standing near the entrance to the last meadow before the road, beyond which an old mill marked the end of the valley. He was pale, very nervous, and his voice caught in his throat.

"The fields turn up there before the road," he said. "There are two meadows below. She's not there."

"Then she's crossed the stream," said Edmond. "And if she's crossed, it's at the Pêchoire, that's the only place."

"And the road? What if she crossed the road?"

"What do you think she's going to do there? That's gardens."

"She could do anything, that cow. And the dog doesn't even understand what we want. She thinks we're playing."

"We're going to cross the stream," said Alice, seeing Adrien turn gray with anxiety. "All four of us will move forward in a line between the trees and the road until we reach the plain up there."

"I'm afraid she might have fallen into the pits," said Adrien, trembling.

Between the mill and the Noue, the stream widened many times to form coves without banks, very deep, where the water darkened, where the current seemed to be still. Children weren't allowed to play near them.

"Oh no," said Albert. "First of all, cows are very good swimmers."

"But if she's broken a leg?"

"She would moo."

They crossed over the ruined pilings that might have once been the Pêchoire bridge, where the stream was shallow enough for Roussette to have considered attempting it. Then all four ran in a line over the path. A long time later, Rosa, who was beginning to get nervous, stood up and saw them arriving from the other side of the stream, silent, followed by the dog who was trotting along behind. Adrien was white as a sheet.

"You haven't got her," Rosa noticed.

"No, nothing."

"I've lost my cow," said Adrien.

Dismayed, all the others knew that his misfortune could be their own.

"We're all to blame," said Rosa. "We weren't keeping watch."

"All the same, it's my cow," said Adrien.

"What are we going to do?"

"It's high time we got back," said Rosa. "We're already late."

Knowing infallibly when it was time to go home, all the herds had already gathered behind her. It was late. The sun had set a long time ago.

"What do you want us to do, Adrien?" asked Albert gently.

Adrien seemed lost. His frightened look passed from one of them to another, and then it paused for a long time on the drawn little face of Alice, whose eyes widened. All of a sudden, he seemed to make up his mind.

"We're all going to go back. You, Albert, your route passes our house. I'm going to follow you, just behind you. When we reach the gate, you'll let my cows and goats in. This time of day, it's open and either my father or my mother is in the barnyard. Okay?"

"Why don't you want to do it yourself?"

"Because I want to come right back down. You only have to tell my father or mother that Roussette is lost and I'm looking for her. I'd rather have you be the one who tells them, you understand?"

"You're right," said Edmond. "That way, you'll avoid getting smacked. But your parents are going to come down, too."

"You think so?"

"You bet! Don't you realize? This is a cow!"

"Come on, let's go," said Rosa. "If we don't, we're all going to get smacked."

"Others besides your parents will come to help, too," said Albert. "My brother will come for sure, or my grandfather."

"Maybe Maria," said Adrien.

"And my father, too," said Edmond. "Come on, let's go home."

The children helped the dogs separate out the herds, which all wanted to leave together, and began to organize them to get them across the ford. Adrien drew Alice aside by the sleeve. His face frightened the little girl.

"You're all gray," she said. "Adrien, listen to me! You're not going to throw yourself into the pits?"

The boy's teeth were clenched.

"He's going to beat me," he said. "The cow is lost. They won't be able to find it any more than we could, or else they'll find it dead. He'll kill me."

"Are you crazy? Adrien, are you crazy? He's your father."

"No, he's not really my father. He beat me for a swollen cow. For a dead cow, what will he do to me? But I have a gun. I'm going to defend myself. I'll defend myself to the death, you hear? To the death. There's no one but you, you and Maria. You have to help me."

He put his arm around her neck and whispered into her ear for a long time. The little girl listened, frozen with fear, nodding her head, discovering an Adrien in revolt whom she didn't know. Edmond's voice drew them apart.

"Alice, come on!" he cried. "Rosa's gone, follow your cows, they're crossing with your dog, your goats are in front."

Adrien saw the small silhouette hurry off behind the animals and disappear down the path into the woods just where the wood anemones were fading. Behind Rosa, Edmond's whole herd had already crossed the ford.

"So we'll do what you said?" called Albert.

"That's right. Don't forget, Albert."

"Let's go!"

Adrien crossed the ford last, pushing the goats. On the last stone, he turned around. Darkened by evening, the Noue was empty. Choked by the dam, the current ran with a soft purr, which the silent mills obeyed. Engulfed by the lonely stream, the game no longer belonged to anyone but him.

Having reached the road, Adrien was seized with a feeling of intense helplessness when he saw the house. He stopped, letting the herd and Sirène go on without him. Enclosed up until then in the intimate community of the Noue, his misfortune was going to clear the fence and leave the world of the children. And in some confused way, it was this other world, even more than his father's anger, that he was going to have to face, the world of norms, laws, faults weighed and dealt with, the world of crimes and cut-off heads, of suffocations, of accusations and punishments, before which he had no one to defend him since those accusations and punishments would come from the very ones who could stand up for him. Even if Roussette was found again, his wrongdoing would remain as great as if she had drowned in the pits. He saw his herd sweep through the entrance and take over the barnyard. Albert kept his word. He went in, too, and talked with the silhouette of Clémence. This image was like a turning key: it locked Adrien into a citadel of solitude where his only defenses henceforth would be the hideout and the gun.

His saw the silhouette of his mother waving her arms, and then that of his father approaching, but before he had run to catch up with his animals, he had also fled as fast as he could. He hesitated at the crossroads where one road led to Maria's house, but didn't take it, and then continued through the Bastière and slowed down so that the loud noise of his clogs didn't betray him. Walking carefully, he reached the gate of Alice's house. She wasn't there. He stood in the shadows, his back to one of the pillars, looking into the yard, where a farmhand was watering the horse. Now an apprehension very different from fear knotted his belly, even though he was sure that Alice would come. Soon he saw her thin profile outlined in the lit-up door frame of the house. Despite the darkness, he could make out the little red checks of her dress. For a moment, her face appeared in the full light, and Adrien felt a strong sensation of sweetness and despair run through him, like bloody tears. Alice came nonchalantly into the yard as though out for a stroll, crossed imperceptibly toward the gate, skipped as if playing hopscotch, and went out to the road.

"Here," she said.

She handed him a little package wrapped in a rag, which he grabbed and stuck in his pocket.

"I'm scared," said Alice.

"Don't I know it!"

"And what if we told everything?"

"What do you mean everything?"

"The gun, the lead shot. And that you saw the murderer running."

"It's too late, it's much too late."

"But I'm sure your father wouldn't beat you."

"It's not just my father I'm afraid of. He'll find out. It's every-one, the whole world. I'll never be able to watch the animals again. I won't be good for anything, anything!"

"But what are you going to do over there? It's nighttime, you haven't eaten!"

"I don't know. I'll defend myself. Everyone must know. It's the only way."

The little girl listened, finding her friend hard and determined, refusing everything, this boy who ordinarily wanted so much to be loved. She hesitated.

"I'm afraid to go with you."

"No," said Adrien, who felt a mysterious surge of energy that made him stagger. "No, my Alice. I have to be all on my own now. Okay! Off you go quickly."

He saw close to him the gold of those beautiful violet eyes glis-tening through the transparency of tears. Abruptly, he took off into the shadow of the road and headed downhill running. He took the stone path and immediately had to slow down. The moon had not yet risen, the path was dark, and he had lost his stick. When the hedge came to an end, he saw the yellow flames of Baromé's fire in front of his caravan. Around them, in a great bubble of light, the shadow of Malvina bustled about and seemed much closer than in the daytime. Muffling his steps, Adrien left behind that reassuring image, after which point the village no longer existed. An inexorable blade now suddenly cut him off from all, in the exclusion of condemnation, for which Roussette, the cow, might have been the trigger, or perhaps the dead kid goat, or that terribly strong desire he had had in the hideout to undress Alice, or the shame that haunted him of being afraid of his father, or those ancient and confused frustrations of pride.

He found the moon again at Pont-Bertrand. This was his first time alone at night in the country, and he was suddenly seized with another anguish, as if he had become the target of enemies waiting in ambush in the huge dark patches that closed him in, enemies to whom he offered himself simply by walking, since their immobility rendered them invisible. The moonlight, on which he had counted for help, on the contrary made the empty meadows more strange, as well as the mass of hedges and the solidity of the tall trees that seemed to have taken off their peaceful daytime masks to reveal their menacing truth. The harmony of the day became a conspiracy by night, hatched by the ironic smirk of the moon. With everything around ready to leap out at him, Adrien was escorted by strange whistling sounds, similar to when the blacksmith plunges red-hot iron into water, mixed with the distant yapping of unknown beasts, the sudden flapping of wings absorbed by the darkness, and then long pitfalls of silence.

He stopped at the bridge and leaned on the parapet, but below him was only a black hole, except for a frozen gray cloth flickering at the washing place like some unintelligible signal. He knew that a very deep pit opened at the base of the bridge, and another Adrien who seemed to split off from him encouraged him to throw himself in. The inextricable web of violence that had ensnared him would be rent with a single blow, the water would swallow him in its peaceful prison. But the Adrien who watched with wild eyes saw once more the gay and stubborn mill wheels turning below the dam. He left the stone bridge, straightened up far from this nocturnal mouth ready to snatch him up, and forced himself to make his clogs sound along the road. Immediately afterward, he entered the gloomy tunnel of elms that led him to the Champarnaud gate.

Great patches of matte white divided the shadows for which he could now name every form. Even though the silent, empty field no longer seemed to belong to the world he knew, he regained his nerve and walked into the meadow up to the ash tree in the middle of the great pale lakes that marked it. He sat down on the stone in a stillness that soon made him one with the night. He was no longer afraid of anything but his own adventure and the storm that he had set off over there. Maybe they had all already headed down into the Noue, which you could see only from the top of the stubble fields, near the tongue of the copse cutting into it. He was reluctant to leave the friendly darkness of the ash tree, but he had to clear the wall, jump over the little hedge, and follow the path. Below him, the smooth surface of the washing place extended out in little glimmering ripples. Lost at the bottom of the landscape, the great flat basin of the Noue was not the darkest part of it. Something was moving there, little dots of yellow light that turned out to be lanterns shifted about. Moving farther off, some of them grew weaker and then disappeared, engulfed by the night. They were calling, too. He heard noises, dogs barking, very muffled, cut regularly by a long call, though its purpose he couldn't make out. It might be him they were calling, and he suddenly caught a glimpse of the commotion for which he was the cause and the center. But whether or not they had found Roussette, he had gone too far to go back now. If they were going to find him, it wouldn't be without a struggle.

He turned over under the ash tree and crawled into the moss house, his mind in a turmoil, his belly tight with a pain he couldn't name. He didn't understand very well how what he had done had led him here, nor what the stakes were in this war. He stayed there a long time, one hand grasping his knife, the other Alice's packet, and little by little, his whole experience simplified itself and the wildness of his rebellion fell into order. He needed to organize himself, to prepare. The moss walls took on their fragility again, giving him no protection against discovery, offering him no shelter if he slept. The only safe place was the hideout. He slipped in there, setting off sudden flights that petrified him. The hazy moonlight, dimmed by the tangle of leaves, hardly lit the chamber hollowed out in the black mass of woods, but the place was so familiar he took heart. The pathetic stick muskets of his childhood were there, pointed toward the valley. Danger could come only from the narrow pass cut in the vegetation to the opening of the field. He set out on his hands and knees, discovered, wrapped in its rags, that threatening weapon that had killed two men, unwrapped it, and took the packet with six of Alice's father's cartridges out of his pocket. It was the same caliber. He slipped two cartridges into the barrels, closed the gun with a snap, and, as if he wanted to prove to himself that he knew how to use it, pushed the safety lock. He sat down, absolutely resolved. The gun froze his hands. There was nothing to do but wait. He entered his first night as an outlaw.

"Damned rotten kid! Now there he goes losing his cow! I'm going to box his ears, you see if I don't!"

Fernand's reaction had not been gentle. Of course he had to go find her, that cow, leaving the stable to Clémence, to take a hurricane lamp, a lead rope, a stick, to whistle for the dog.

"Go on, quick!" Clémence had said. "The little one is all alone out there."

He was going through the gate when Albert's grandfather arrived. He had his lantern, too.

"So, Fernand, looks like you could use some help?"

"Well, the more, the better, Monsieur Mainson."

Fernand had hardly finished thanking him than Henri Mousset arrived with Edmond and Titan.

"You'll be out a good bottle of wine when we've found that cow of yours," said Henri. "My big idiot there, I'm sure he doesn't know how to manage his dog. Where do we start?"

"By the poplars in the Noue. Between there and Pont-Bertrand it's all closed off. She's got to be on the other side."

"So let's go," said Albert's grandfather, "let's find her before supper."

"Adrien must be there, too," said Edmond timidly.

"That rotten little dog!" said Fernand, closing the gate, "his butt's going to sting! That's how he watches that cow, even as unpredictable as she is. Not to mention the trouble he's causing all of you."

"It's not so serious," said Albert's grandfather. "Your Adrien is a good little kid, Fernand. You never played, yourself, when you were watching cows at his age?"

"Calm down," said Henri while they walked along, "his punishment is to be all alone in the valley, and that it's night already."

"Well, I guess you're right," said Fernand, laughing.

His anger retreated, driven away by the pleasure this prompt assistance from his neighbors brought him. He hadn't been drinking for two days, and this kind of immediate support without his weakness being an issue gave him a sort of pride. They spread out in a line along the barbed wire by the poplars and moved forward, sending their dogs off ahead. They regrouped to cross over the hedge, spread out again, crossed the Etranglon meadow where the stream came nearly to the base of the slope, and heard Sirène and Titan barking close to the Charconnier road. Roussette was there, calm, facing off with the dogs. The moment Fernand slipped the lead rope around her neck, they saw the light of a cigarette glow in the darkness.

"You don't have a very good shepherd, Jublin," said a voice.

"Who's there?" said Fernand, moving forward and raising his lantern. "Oh! It's you, Clovis? What are you doing there?"

"Let's just say that I'm waiting," said the voice. "Because you're going to have to supply me with cabbages and salad greens. Your cow has cleaned out my garden," said Clovis Moinet, breaking into laughter.

Coming out of the old mill, he had seen that cow peacefully devastating his garden patch. It was already too late. She must have made her rounds in the thickets above, she had missed a small field of sainfoin and instead found the entrance to the garden. It wasn't a big deal, he had arrived in time to chase Roussette to the village meadows and had waited for them to come looking for her. Fernand thanked him and offered to compensate him, but it was out of the question: for three cabbages and four head of lettuce, it wasn't worth the trouble, a bottle of wine when he came up to the village was fine. They all joked around for a moment as they rolled cigarettes, while Edmond, overjoyed, took Roussette, and then Moinet left them. The whole business was turning out all right.

"Good," said Fernand, "now we just have to find the boy."

"We should have already seen him," said Henri.

"Yes, that's true. Where can he have gone?"

"Jeez! Without a lantern, let's hope that..."

"No, no," said Albert's grandfather. "It's a bright moon, and your son knows this whole area like the back of his hand."

"Even so! Damn it, we're going to go along the pits with lanterns. He should have found Moinet before we did."

"He must have gone up toward the plain," said Edmond, "because we'd already searched there."

Suddenly Fernand called out Adrien's name as loud as he could, the light mist of early night softening the echo.

"Even if he heard you," said Edmond, "he wouldn't come right away. He's afraid of you."

"Of me?"

"Sure, that's why he led his animals up to your gate and took off after sending Albert in to talk to you."

"What's this now! My son, afraid of me! He came all the way to the gate?"

"You must have trounced him a little too hard once," said the grandfather. "Kids, they're like young dogs, they don't forget the strap."

"Afraid of me," said Fernand thoughtfully, "my God!"

"Up to the gate," said Edmond, "he worked it out with Albert."

"All the same, we're going to call him as we go back."

"And call out that we have Roussette."

They followed along the pits lit up by the moon, without finding the least trace, calling out Adrien's name at intervals. At the Pêchoire, Fernand, whose face looked ghostly in the low gleam of his lantern, made up his mind.

"I'm going up to the plain. You, Henri, I don't want to tell you what to do, but if you could go by way of the Outremont with your son?"

"I'll stay below," said Albert's grandfather. "Give me the cow. And we'll all meet up again at Pont-Bertrand."

He arrived there first and sat down quietly on one of the milestones. He waited a long time. From every side of him, far enough from the valley that it wasn't an echo, he heard the tense voice of Fernand calling, sometimes masked by Edmond's shrill cry.

"What do you want us to do, Fernand?" he asked when they had met up again.

"The Noue is empty," said Henri. "Do you want someone to go on the other side of the road to Puypouzin? To the lower bridge? In any case, Monsieur Mainson, your soup will be cold."

"I'm not so worried about that anymore," said the grandfather.

"You know, if he is in the valley or the hills, he's heard you. If he wants to come home, he'll come home."

"You're right," said Fernand. "Maybe he's home already."

"Who knows what goes on in the heads of children," said the grandfather.

Clémence's face was distorted with worry. Seated at the table across from her husband, she had pushed away her plate and was staring into space at a fuzzy image, that of her son lost out in the night, like a representation of the terrible failure that was her life. She thought she guessed what had driven the child to running away. Fernand, somber, had eaten a plate of soup and drank half a glass of wine. His fingers tightened around the glass as if he wanted to crush it. It was late. They had talked a lot, more than they had for a very long time, and had resolved to try to do nothing until morning. Fernand thought that there would still be time to alert the police if Adrien hadn't shown up. As soon as it was day, he would ask Maria to accompany them—the boy loved her so—and if he heard them, maybe he would come. Old Mainson would come too—he had suggested it. As they headed toward Puypouzin, they would also call on Lortier.

"And what if he's had an accident?" said Clémence.

Fernand considered that practically impossible. It was a clear night. For Adrien to fall into the pits, he would have had to really want to do it. But Adrien would certainly have had to sit down or lie down to sleep; they just had to find out where. Maybe in Lortier's barn, above the house, toward Nègressauve, or in the Champarnaud woods, which he knew so well, or near the Fontmaillot spring, where certain rocks overhung some kinds of caves. They would go to all those places the next day, calling out that all was well, that Roussette had been found, that he wouldn't be punished, that they were waiting for him at school.

"Luckily, I put his scarf in his bag," said Clémence.

She had placed a plate of soup, well covered, on the hearthstone, prepared the pâté that he loved, and a jar of peaches in syrup that he would only have to open. It would do no good to wait up; leaving the door unbolted was enough.

"If we hear him come in," said Fernand, "we won't say anything. He'll go up to bed all alone and tomorrow morning we'll do everything just as usual."

For the first time in months, they went into their bedroom together, and Fernand heard his wife say prayers in a low voice as she undressed. With the switch hanging over the bed, he turned out the lights and they both remained there in the dark, silent, listening. Much later, Clémence noticed that Fernand kept swallowing hard, and then he let out continuous little sighs, like sobs. All of a sudden he turned toward her. He spoke with difficulty, as though something was choking him.

"Clémence," he said, "the little one was afraid of me."

"It could be," she said.

"Listen, Clémence, it's because of me, it's my drinking. I know that well enough. And for you, too, I know it. This will be the end of that drinking now. Don't cry, Clémence. I can't stand it that my son is afraid of me. I want it to be like it was before."

"It isn't too late?" whispered Clémence. "Can you do it?"

"Oh yes, I can do it. You have to help me. Our little one has to be here."

Never had Adrien imagined that the night could be so long. He had heard the calling again, this time on the Outremont. He had made out his name, but that was from the other side of the road. Then everything fell silent again. He was able to prop his gun in one of the forks. Freed of the gun, he could rub his frozen hands and his bare legs, which had grown stiff. The woods were alive around him. Something gliding through the leaves made them rustle very lightly. From behind the hideout, always in the same place, came a regular gnawing sound, as something chewed away at its prey. He was too afraid to sleep. He shifted positions only very slowly, so that nothing gave away his presence to all the wild beasts and maybe also to the serpents who took shelter in these woods. Hunger was a vague contraction in his belly, so mixed up with the knot of fear that he didn't feel it as hunger, but he had a terrible thirst. He had walked a lot and felt weary and thirsty. He had to keep himself from thinking about water. He told himself that in the morning, early, before there was any danger, he would go down along the woods to the stream to drink there and wash his face as he did in his basin. This image called up his room, the table with his books, the wall he had decorated with the weapons Fernand had found. His teacher had said that the ax was no doubt Oriental and that the lance was called a *guisarme,* a word that delighted him.

He imagined his notebook hidden on the beam. It would certainly take him many pages to write down what had happened. Then suddenly he understood that he could no longer write in that notebook, nor go back to his room, that he was banished from everything, that this night spent here in the cold was a definitive break in his life that he had not fully measured, and he was terrified by it. He could hardly sort out what had led him to this. He had wanted to combat a punishment, and more than that, the reprobation that, because of a single fault, found him no longer capable of anything, ending all hopes anyone had for him. And now he wondered if his running away didn't give weight to those reproaches he'd wanted to fend off. He didn't know where the path he had started down led, maybe nowhere. But what he wanted from the dead future was for people to know that he existed, on welfare or not, that he hated this village where they killed baby goats. He was afraid of entering into the world of men, but in his hands he held a weapon that could make them afraid, too. It could go off if it had to—that's what it was made for—and he knew how to use it. The perverse odor of the gun, the strange pleasure of its contact, and the vague desire to embrace Alice suddenly gave him an unsuspected virility to which his male body responded for the first time.

Soon the cold was stronger than his fear. He moved, crawled through the passage regardless of what he awoke, and reached the field. He dismantled the house of dry moss, brought back an armful of it, carpeted the floor of the hideout, and covered his legs. He was shivering. He was living an eternity with no way out. For a long time, he slipped into a sleepy torpor, from which he was abruptly awakened by two yellowish white spots, two brilliant eyes that stared at him from behind the ash shoots and terrified him. He leaped back instinctively to save himself, bumped into some branches, and felt an emptiness inside that devoured him, but before he was able to grab the gun, the eyes had run off into a hardly perceptible break in the woods. It had the agility of a fox—a badger would walk more heavily.

The moon was down, making it very dark now. No, the gun was real. He was confronting real dangers that did nothing to tame his secret violence, but that made him a little boy again, very little, minuscule in this enormous night where everything was alive. He wondered if it would end, if what he was doing there would end. And suddenly an immense sorrow overcame him, a wave that had waited a long time to break and now drowned him in tears. He wiped them with his sleeve. He tried to weep silently, but big hiccups shook him, and irrepressible sobs and sniffles made him bury his face in his arms, wrapped around his knees. Finally his tears ran dry, the last ones still leaving their stiff traces on his cheeks. He lay down on the moss, exhausted but free of his anguish, timidly reconciled with the night. Above his roof of branches, he saw a very bright star, finally, a friendly gleam that reassured him. With the first rays of dawn, he was submerged by sleep.

That was his name. From very far away, he heard someone calling him, and then his name was suddenly called out nearby. In an instant, he reawoke to the bright day, the hideout, his story. He jumped. It was in the field. It was the voice that he would punish. He grabbed the gun with both hands, pushed the safety catch. The voice approached, terrifying, crying his name. A terrible explosion threw him to the ground; there was a blaze, a violent shock against his hip, and then the insidious odor, the intoxicating spell of powder and death, the captivating odor of death, a dizzying silence.

"Are you crazy?" shouted the voice. "Adrien, are you crazy? Have you got a gun?"

He heard running feet and the cry, "Bloody hell! He's got a gun!" Then the voice took up again, farther away. Now it must have been at the Champarnaud gate.

"It's not possible. Adrien, listen, it's not possible. Roussette's been found, but that doesn't matter. It's my fault, I know it is. I won't drink anymore. My son, I have to tell you, the farm, the fields, the animals, none of it matters without you. Come, let me have that gun."

There was a long silence again, and then the voice said only, "Adrien!" and stopped. Nothing moved. He heard steps going away down the path. He got to his knees. His whole body ached, and he no longer knew if he were really awake, but as soon as he opened the gun, the enchanting odor assured him of it. He had fired, and nevertheless he was sure he hadn't wanted to kill his father, no, only to put the obstacle of the weapon out before him, to tell him it was there. He felt like he was half dreaming, very far away from everything, as if he had reached another world where nothing remained but the desire to be lying in his room waiting for his mother's kiss. He was hugging Alice. He was by the sea with Maria. He was drawing maps. He and his father were both sitting on top of a cartload of hay, coming home singing "The Brave Sailor." He looked out at the infinite expanse of land from Champarnaud. His only escape appeared as a glaring truth: he had to kill himself.

He took out the empty cartridge and closed the gun again over the second one. The hideout was nothing anymore, only a reminder of the nocturnal horror. He needed the day, the light. When he came out of the woods, the sun striking the steel of the barrel blinded him for an instant. He saw the peaceful and indifferent field again. Despite his aching body, he managed to climb over the wall, jump the hedge, and follow the little path. The valley was huge. Way at the bottom, near the washing place, a little group was looking up in his direction, Albert's grandfather was pointing at him with his stick. Clémence's two fists were pressed over her mouth. Maria raised her arm and waved. He took a few steps along the thickets that cut into the stubble fields up to the meadows, when his father appeared—walking in front of Lortier, to whom he was talking— half turned around, until he, too, looked up and saw him.

His father called him. Maria called him. He felt that the slope was gradually drawing his body down. In the middle of the stubble field, he could no longer stop himself, the incline carried him with it. He held the gun in one hand and ran. He saw the ones who were approaching, frozen before him as he came hurtling down and jumped over the lower wall, running. He saw them flee, crouch with their hands over their heads, lie down flat on their stomachs. Only his father came toward him, his arms wide open, transfigured by happiness. Everything was closing in on him so quickly that he was no longer in control of it, but he had to kill himself there, he had to do it now. He saw all the faces, all the eyes wide with fear, except his father's, who was smiling, his arms open. Swept up in his fervor, he managed to take the gun in his other hand, raise it toward himself, savagely pull the trigger. With a thunderous roar, the gun jumped, ringing against the underwater stones of the washing place. The shot sprayed out from the other side into the poplars, out of which flew a light cloud of shredded leaves. Adrien, gasping for breath, trembling all over, fell into his father's arms. He felt the rough jacket, the warm smell, the protection of Fernand, who hugged him, murmuring, "My little one, it's all over, it's all over." When his mother, disfigured by a fear she hadn't yet been able to drive away, pulled him out of Fernand's arms to hug him frantically, Adrien finally understood that he wasn't dead. Maybe everything could start over once again.

XII

lortier

EARLY IN THE MORNING, closing the little valley gate, Lortier gradually concealed behind one of the thick doors the image of his happiness: over there, in front of the house, Mo was folding a sheet with one of her girls and both of them were laughing because one of them had pulled too hard at the wrong time on the folded cloth, and the other had let it go; behind them a very old rosebush was studded with white blossoms, and the structure of the arbor bending into the flower and vegetable gardens marked off a verdant foreground. At the center, the brilliant whiteness of the sheet contrasted dramatically with the golden stone of the old walls and seemed to reflect the sun into Mo's gray hair so she appeared blond. This timeless scene erased forever the wars, the murders, and the cruelties that the fortified house had withstood. Lortier gently closed the door again behind him, as though to protect it.

He took the path and, before setting off on the little road above the stubble fields, turned around. The house was only the organization into walls and roofs of primitive rock gradually assembled to bring it into existence. It had a powerful knowledge of time and Lortier suddenly knew with incontestable clarity that he was only a transient guest, one summer's leaf on a very old tree. That was really how it was. He had lived as a nomad quite a bit, stubbornly searching for the first signs of his own species buried beside African lakes or on the Andes plateaus or surviving in the Siberian reindeer hunters' frozen plains, but the tenacious Poitou peasantry had recaptured him by some roundabout means and held him there. All he had to do was slip humbly into that old stronghold, to mold himself to it, to make it accept the tools of his own times with his presence. He and it were hosts or guests, both words stemming from the same root. But looking at time another way, the house sheltered only the fleeting wanderings of one passing through. Nevertheless, when in the middle of the night he waited for sleep, she sometimes allowed him to become the heart of it, her guardian, this vast womblike and nurturing vessel of which he knew each limb, as he gazed about him, through walls and doors from one room to another, from the beams of the turret to the depths of the cellars, in a miraculous silence.

Putting on the canvas backpack he had brought along to bring Mo the bread she wanted, he walked to the first drystone wall. Below him, the valley sparkled. The fixed whiplash of the stream took on the icy black of leather, which turned a hemp gray where it wasn't lined by trees. The stationary poplar groves, the meadows hardly delineated by the fences, the jumbled skeleton of rock denting the thin stubble fields—it all had the trembling motionlessness of a silent prayer. Lortier couldn't say why this landscape, with its vista of vague distances that he could nevertheless decipher into their smallest contours, always had such a magical harmony for him. He didn't know how this harmony gradually penetrated him until he became one of its elements, converging with all the others in a kind of primary order, eternal and sovereign, below which the frenzy of the world disappeared. You are very argumentative this morning. Just be happy to welcome the beauty of June on your skin.

He continued following the small road, crossed through the woods cutting into the stubble fields much farther on, and stopped at the spot Adrien had stood while he had watched him, motionless, just before he had rushed down the slope. It hadn't been easy to speak afterward, no one could find the right words. The shot had shredded Adrien's earlobe, covering his face and neck with blood. From hugging him, Fernand had gotten himself all red. Seeing the two of them looking like Indians in war paint, Maria had suddenly burst into nervous laughter and everything was resolved. Maria had washed them with her handkerchief while old Mainson hiccuped from laughing. Clémence had torn off the bottom of her slip, and as she tried awkwardly to bandage the boy's ear, she, too, began to laugh through her tears, interrupting herself sometimes to hug him violently to her. Fernand, smiling, watched Adrien intently. They all stopped laughing to let out big sighs.

"Good," Fernand had said suddenly, "now we won't talk about it anymore, it's over."

"I brought you some pâté sandwiches," said Clémence, but Adrien shook his head no. His hunger still hadn't returned. He was having a lot of trouble coming back from his distant voyage.

"Do you agree, Monsieur Mainson?" said Fernand. "We won't talk about it anymore? No one is to hear about this!"

"Okay," Albert's grandfather had said. "May the devil strike me. Not Albert or anyone else."

"We'll go to La Rochelle," said Maria, "your mother says it's fine."

"I've been to see your teacher," said Clémence. "I said that you were a little tired. They are all waiting for you."

"Good!" Fernand had said. "I might have shot in my cheek, I think. It's burning. No need to stand around here, eh? Are we waiting for the grass to grow?"

"Okay, let's go!" the grandfather had said. "Maria and I by the stone path of the Bastière, you by the stubble fields, you go back by the garden. Who's going to take care of the gun?"

"Me," Lortier had said, "leave that to me."

He would have liked to take Adrien along with him, and he knew that Maria, too, had the same desire. They both guessed that Fernand and the boy, by trial and error, would have to tame what they had discovered about what linked them, and no doubt Adrien needed a long rest. At the same time, the freshness of childhood was such that a long night's sleep and a day of school and play might calm and subdue all he had so brutally gone through.

Lortier thought about it again going down to the stream. Death or the instrument signifying it, which he had held in his hand, must have gradually ensnared this child and tempted him with its escape, disguised as deliverance from he didn't know what, maybe simply his childhood. "So now it begins," he said to himself. "Just when the darkness greets me, the morning comes and also the night; Zacharie read that in his Bible." What mattered at present wasn't to explain but to plan. Lortier had made an agreement with Fernand that the boy should come learn drawing with Mo. He would take advantage of that opportunity to suggest books to him, and Mo and Maria would be glad to be able to shower him with even more tender affections, this boy who, if he were a few years older, could have been one of his grandsons.

He stopped by the washing place and was surprised by his shortness of breath, since the descent should have made his walking easy. This was where he had recovered the gun, on the flagstones where the lively water ran. He had dried it without cleaning the barrels. He had wiped off all marks, had been careful to also wipe the fired cartridge that he had left there, and had taken the weapon to the police. They had verified the number. It really was Germain Brunet's. Someone had found it there where Brunet said it was hidden and had gotten rid of it by throwing it into the stream. Two meters farther down, the gun fell to the bottom of the Pont-Bertrand pit to lie dormant there for years, and the police were very satisfied with how everything had turned out.

Lortier sat down on the milestone where carts bringing the laundry for large washings were tied. His mind was empty of thoughts as he watched the running water, fascinated by its shimmering. He was hot, and he felt so sluggish that he had a moment's desire to turn back, to stretch out in his easy chair, but he had to take his revenge on what he hadn't the courage to face on his last walk. How short it was, this life, although it still didn't end up being new! He rose with the help of his walking stick, chose to follow the stream, crossed the water at the ford in the middle, but didn't take the path that he would have followed to the basket makers. He didn't feel he had the heart for conversation. He cut diagonally across the slope of the hillside, concentrating on breathing slowly and deeply, without paying too much attention to his heart beating in his chest. Inexplicably, he saw the image of his children, who were smiling at him, not as they were now, at forty or fifty, but younger, varied, all bearing their character in their expression, smiling at him all together. And it was like an unexpected gift, a sudden blessing bestowed upon him. He felt a great joy that welled up in him, burned, broke into stars with flaming, intersecting trajectories—a mass of suns blurring the image from which they seemed to come under the wheel of great scathing rays—and then everything disappeared.

He found himself lying in the grass, sliding so as not to roll down the slope, sharply aware of the dizzy spell that had landed him there. The vise that gripped his arm slowly relaxed. He was very warm. He hadn't let go of his stick. He planted it in the ground, hauled himself up, and straightened. He let the storm pass, driving it out of himself in long measured breaths, as though he were using a bellows, taking care not to extinguish the small flames he wanted to rekindle. Everything was all right now, he was only tired and thirsty, but Puypouzin was a long way off. The roofs of the first houses of the Bastière stood in a line behind the ridge. He decided to stop by at Zacharie's.

The door of the workshop was open and the carpenter was washing his hands outside in an old sink that caught rainwater over the tangle of little fossils embedded in its stone.

"You've dropped in at a good time," he said. "I've just finished planting my leeks. I'm late. Leeks should be planted in early May. Which do you prefer, the house or workshop?"

"The workshop."

"Then go in and sit down wherever you can, I'm going to get a small bottle of Pomerol and two glasses. Wait a minute, look at me.

What happened to you? You look funny and your face is all gray. Don't you feel well?"

"I walk on those slopes too much. The climb is too much for me."

"What if I give you a little glass of three-six?"

"No, not that! It would spoil your Pomerol for me. Bring me a big glass of water, too," he called to Zacharie, who had taken off running.

The smell of the wood made Lortier feel at peace with himself. He sat down on a toolbox. Zacharie must have suddenly thought of his leeks and left the work that was under way. Posts of light yellow, subtly veined ash were resting on the workbench strewn with wood shavings. He wondered why manual work moved him so, maybe because he had unearthed stone or bone tools everywhere that bore the mark of his species, and from which everything had followed. He loved nothing so well as the noble look in the eye of the artisan speaking passionately about his craft. Zacharie knew how to be servant and master to his wood. He envied him. All his life, Lortier had applied his archaeologist's mind to puzzling out, and sometimes comprehending, the ancient gestures that had ensured that triumphant duality over everything, over the three kingdoms and the four elements. What purpose had his efforts served? He had no idea. The brain was a beautiful tool, too, though not necessarily put to good use.

Zacharie appeared in the doorway, carrying in one hand the glass he held out to him, in the other the bottle, which he placed on the workbench with the two glasses he drew out of his pocket. Lortier drank the water in big thirsty swallows. Over the steel-rimmed glasses he must have put on to uncork the bottle, Zacharie's good worried eyes looked at him hard.

"Feeling better? You scared me with that Lazarus-back-from-the-grave face of yours," he said, smiling. "What was it?"

"I had a little spell of faintness climbing Piémont, but it's passed. Your Pomerol is going to put me back in the saddle."

"Okay, cheers!" said Zacharie, clinking glasses. "The one who lives without some madness isn't as wise as he thinks, that's for sure. But say, my man, aren't you doing a little too much maybe? You're getting to the age when the candles cost more than the cake."

"Now see here, my man! And what could I say about you?"

"You could say that I don't have a game leg and that I don't wander all about the countryside."

"It doesn't bother me," said Lortier, "it's only higher up that that happens."

He had had worse luck than Zacharie. The war had damaged one of his legs, which sometimes became heavy and painful, but it wasn't obvious. He raised his glass cheerfully as if he had toasted again. The Pomerol was honest, strong, delicious. With it, all his strength returned.

"You can't guess what a lovely fish I found the day before yesterday in the Pont-Bertand washing place, under thirty centimeters of water: Germain Brunet's gun."

Zacharie was astounded. "Bravo," Lortier said to himself, "old Mainson was able to hold his tongue." He talked about his discovery and what he had done with it.

"That's the work of a snoop," said Zacharie, "or of a kid who was snaring birds in those woods. He found the contraption where that dog hid it, and when he saw what it was, after a few days, he got rid of it in a good place, so that those doing their wash would find it. Do you know, it's almost embarrassing to go get a shave now? Cécile just cries. He won't be punished for that, but he's wrecked his wife's life too."

The ruined lives, the madness of the murders, the child, Adrien, his own children who had carried him away, and now the carpenter's camaraderie made Lortier suddenly make up his mind.

"Your wine warms my heart, Zacharie," he said, "but listen, I have to talk to you. I have to talk. All the time now, I keep turning my life over in my mind. There are not only beautiful sides to it. I feel bad, because, to tell the truth, I've lacked courage."

"Oh, come now," said Zacharie calmly.

"I have shadows, which I have always despised, but they are there. And I've gotten along all right with them. Good student, good soldier, good husband, good father, good archaeologist, there, that's the song of the lark, but often I've felt like the sparrow hawk. Sometimes I've had the desire to destroy everything, to change everything, to flee, but it was too late, or too difficult for me. Everyone thought I was humble when I was bursting with pride. My lark loved the success and the honors reassured her, and my sparrow hawk would have liked to kill her for that. I've often fooled my world. I've played at being mature and sure of myself, when I was really childish and uncertain. You think I've had a resolved, straightforward life, while, for me, it's been without coherence. I'm coming to the end and I no longer know very well what I am. Don Quixote dies wise after having lived mad; for me, it's the opposite."

"What's this you're telling me?" Zacharie cut in gently. "You know that if you said all you've just said to me to your wife, she might be angry? Your life with her has been incoherent? When she has only lived for you? And you find all that uncertain?"

"Ah!" said Lortier, caught off guard, "but it's not that life I'm talking about."

"Because you think there are two of them? Go on!"

He didn't dare say how Zacharie had hit it just right. His love for Mo swept away all the bitterness, all the desires he had had to change his life. She was the wise one and the child, the lark and the sparrow hawk, light and shadow, she ennobled it all. With all women, Lortier's great fear had been of deceiving, in the way that he had always loved the conquest and neglected the plunder, but Mo had ruled over him, had soothed and calmed him, had provided the safest harbor, also offering the secret of that haven into which eternity sometimes slipped. That their bodies were less vigorous than in the past changed nothing. It was still the same fire, consuming or at rest, but always burning, the same insatiable pleasure in walking beside her, in touching her skin. And whether he had been sinner or saint, it made no difference to those moments when something of the infinite arose in him, a sun of glory.

"It's true," he said finally in a contrite tone. "I talk of pride, when it was vanity. I complain of that existence even though it's become secondary in merging with the other."

"What you have there," Zacharie continued, "is a big ego crisis. With all your diplomas and your learned books, you reason like a blockhead. And as for courage, what would I have to say for myself? I know that one wet dog doesn't make another dry, but do you think that I've had courage, me, dreaming my whole life of a dead wife instead of one who could give me children, for whom I'd struggle along with my saw and my plane in order to bring them up? That would have been courage. My Lord, I've known you like I've known the grain of wood. You wanted to be a model of justice, but that isn't often possible for people. And then, what about this story of going over and over your life, of looking into the cemeteries when you have to look far out over the walls! It's today and tomorrow that count."

"Damn it!" said Lortier. "Zacharie, you've made me well, you've revived me. That's as good as three-six."

The carpenter thumped his fist on his workbench.

"There's one word that I don't like in your beautiful speech, and that's 'despise.' We don't have the right to despise anyone, except those who do evil. And you and I, since the war, we haven't wavered on that point. True evil, the devil's evil, is to subjugate others by force, to make others suffer through cruelty, or to kill man or beast for something other than food or self-defense. Your little honors that make you itch, next to this, it's like a nettle sting compared to leprosy."

"You're right," said Lortier, "I'm sorry. It's you who's the just man."

"Oh no! Only my joinery was just, when my eyes were good. But see here! Where have you led me with your nonsense? So you feel all right now?"

"With your two glasses of wine and your sermon, I feel fine."

"Do you want me to go get the mechanic's car to take you home?"

Lortier ably got to his feet, and he still had one or two little stops to make. Before the face of Saint Joseph haloed by the white curls of the old carpenter who embraced him so warmly, he felt at peace again. All the thorns that had torn at him in imagining that he didn't know why or what had been his life in the face of others lost their edge. He was almost ashamed at being so blessed with Mo after what his friend had just confided for the first time, this dead and never forgotten love. Zacharie walked him to the gate. They smiled as they shook hands and took leave of each other.

Lortier had decided to confront the childhood house this time by some other way than the garden. As soon as he saw its facade, he felt a very old familiarity with it, which the house didn't cause but reawoke as sometimes his memories alone did. The sandstone lost in the limestone wall was there as always, the yew tree from which it pumped moisture needed to be pruned, the border of oxalis hadn't been turned under. But what he looked at now had forgotten what he alone knew: the little boy who drew water from the well, the white mare, the dog, the old man whistling or hiding a key in a hole in the scaffolding, or testing his knife blade with a finger, just a gesture—all those ghosts who in order to exist no longer needed this house, now just coldly surviving, except the one that came back to life in him at his pleasure. The garden of asparagus and raspberry bushes, the beehives neatly lined up to the east now slept under the grass, and a tangle of morning glory marked where sparrows used to chirp in the huge pile of straw. "Don't linger in the cemeteries," Zacharie had said, "look far over the walls!" It was a beautiful middle-class house without a memory, and maybe Zélie Madron was spying on him from behind her bay laurel hedge, watching for the least sign

of regret. It was enough to leave behind the still-visible traces of
what he himself had planted, drawn, constructed for the others
who were no longer there. He knocked the ground hard with a
quick tap of his cane and took off.

He ran into Elodie Russeille, healthy and smiling, stopped to
exchange a few words with Paulus, called Carmagnole, in front of
his open shop, who had pushed his cobbler's last from between his
thighs and was resting his leg shod in the big orthopedic boot he'd
made himself, attached to an iron shank to straighten his clubfoot.
Paulus was a cheerful anarchist. He mocked all he would have liked
to strangle. He began the chronicle of the events shaking the world
with greed, but Lortier was well beyond him and cut it short. The
bakery door, as it opened, set ringing the pleasant sound of a little
bell that made a young woman jump. News was exchanged, he
broke his bread in half to put it in his pack, and went out rich with
the gaiety of bright teeth in a cherry mouth, as young as the always
new odor of bread.

"I am old and faded," said Mo, "I wonder what you find in me."
"I find you," he said.

Leaning heavily on his cane, he took the narrow alley descending
between the walls and gardens toward the town hall and the school.
The vise began to grip his shoulder and arm, but more gently, sig-
naling to Lortier only that it was there. He passed the house near
the play school, where his mother had given birth to him, and it
was as if she stood there, near the open door, to welcome him. His
mother had given him a luminous little childhood but had suffered
in seeing him grow up. As he reached adolescence, the devouring
passion grew in her to live for him as she would have wanted him

to live for her, to sacrifice herself for him, even if he had no need of sacrifice. She had gone through agony knowing he was at war and nearly at the same time losing her husband, to the point that it was believed for a time her mind was affected. They had both had violent bursts of love for each other that did not always mesh. The place that his mother had played in his own life was an inextricable web of joys and torments. He didn't want to think about it. Violently, he chased away all the bitter memories, the clashes, the pain. He wanted only to remember the tender moments, those harmonious ones in which they passionately had been mother and son.

Lortier went on without turning around and reached the washing place above. There was no one there. The noise of the spring made him thirsty. With difficulty, he kneeled down on one of the flagstones polished by centuries of washing and drank out of his hand, listening to the running water. It took him a long time to get up again, his heart beat in confusion, and he was in a hurry to get back. A little farther on, the school murmured through its open windows. From one of them, where, no doubt, the younger class was, flew the monotonous chant of many voices, which must have been a lesson recited in chorus. He was touched by the intonations of children, before this new building that didn't erase the courtyard for playing marbles or running races, the lining up for going in, the room with walls hung with maps where his father had taught him grammar and ethics. When it was empty, at the end of the day, he would go there in secret, tasting his exquisite fear. Over there, near the blackboard, protected by the closely arranged tables, the rag hung on its string. Like all the objects hiding their malice and pretending to be asleep during the day, it waited for the darkness to release it from its stationary servitude and animate it with nearly imperceptible palpitations, like the slight beating of silent wings, a cloth bat moving its folds. He was so afraid, and at the same time so determined, that tears came to his eyes as he extended his hand, and then finally grabbed hold of this creature who died between his fingers, soft and limp, fringed with a cloud of white dust like a puff-ball mushroom.

He shook himself, walked faster to get away from the village, nearly oppressed by what flooded back, as if the guardians of his childhood had been let out of its bag. It awaited him again at the village entrance, at the crossing of the main road and the wide stone path that descended to the lower bridge, and it set up a large star platform where the ancient fires of midsummer glowed for him again. It was always very late once the moon rose. His father stuck a piece of firewood on the end of a short fork and put it in his hand. His mother raised the lantern very high and remained on the steps until they had closed the gate again. Happily, they answered the loud greetings from the groups of peasants, more and more numerous as they approached that great glow that warded off the night over there. The bristling shadows of vines danced along the paths. The immense crackling inferno suddenly hit them, shooting sputtering sparks into the darkness; and this royal presence of the fire to which all the restlessness of the countryside dedicated itself plunged him, dumbfounded, into a savage and sumptuous ritual of intoxicating rounds, leaps over the coals, burning and trembling air that tightened the skin till it split. The dragon twisted about, its red tongues darting out. You crowned it with a sheaf of wheat devoured in one breath to purify the next harvest. He collapsed with fatigue coming home on the shoulders of his father, who must have been very young at that time. But for him, rocked back and forth by his steps, his father was the invincible safeguard that no flaming banner, no power of the night, no magic bat could ever make recoil.

He crossed the sunlit platform, washed clean of all night, and set out on the steep climb of the stone path, steadying himself with his cane in the places gullied by winter where pebbles rolled away underfoot. He was breathing hard, unsettled by everything that wouldn't stop hounding him, all these faces whirling around him. His father loved hiding places, underground tunnels, caves, flint glistening in the plowed fields after the rain, silver coins or pottery shards gleaned from the ancient ruins that his digging revealed. He loved to analyze the land, study the geology of soils, look for springs. He was moved by the migration of birds. During the long walks they had taken together much later, he had taught his son, along with the names of plants and the tracks of animals, what he knew about the long adventure of humans and what he hoped for his future. He had died young. Since then, Lortier had always been an orphan.

It was impossible to hurry on this path. He stumbled. All this was mingling together a bit too quickly, and he was no longer master of his head or his feet. A savage fox was devouring his arm once again. Finally he reached the end of the path, took the road, and stopped to rest, sitting down on a milestone at the lower bridge, but now he understood that what was approaching cared neither about walking nor rest. And so, this was it. What he had so often met up with in the war, questioned before thousand-year-old sepulchres, dreamed of on evenings while lying in wait for game or beside Mo after making love, it was here. What had for so long seemed to him overwhelming, opaque, unimaginable, was, besides a vivid pain, this light and impalpable presence that surrounded him in its transparency until it brushed up against him. He had to get back to Mo, to reach her; he absolutely had to.

Determined, he took the path with the steep slope but that cut over quickly to the house, its blue roofs waiting overhead in a magnificent azure sky. Mo merged with the throbbing of his blood, with the stream behind him, with the bunches of mallow and wild chicory in the stubble field. She was his final recourse, where that little underground abyss over which he often leaned was forgotten. "I have lived tragically a happy life," he said to himself. He had traveled with a radiant love; nevertheless, he had secretly dragged along in his wake a blind companion who clung to his sleeve. Cold sun, colorless, windless country, vertigo of absence with its magnetic pull. Unbearable contradiction of his species bringing forth saints and henchmen, and those insatiable warriors. Nevertheless it had sometimes seemed to him in some fleeting way so tenuous that he only became aware of it as it disappeared, that he approached what must be Truth, or what he himself contained of Truth. And in this lightning flash, despite the dead children and ravaged corpses, the world was good; it would have been enough to set straight what was crooked, to amend what was perverse and destructive. But the golden age was only a wing beat grazing the impassive blue sky. He was only an average man, his mark would be minuscule, except in a few hearts.

He shook himself violently, planted his cane before him, and hauled himself up the path. No. No! Death was intolerable.

Everything would continue without him, the flesh of those he loved would live without him, he would be all alone to no longer be, unjustly alone. The true revolt lay there, the walled house would defy all storms, the mallow and wild chicory would begin to bloom again. A stifling suffering gnawed at his chest, which another self seemed to contemplate without being affected by it. His children appeared again in the transparency over the path to the valley gate, over there, so far away. They were happy, Adrien was with them, all his grandchildren surrounded him, pulled him laughing toward the door where Mo leaned out and extended a hand toward him, where his life leaned out toward him but he could no longer grasp anything, and Mo's grief tore him apart. "There is still hope," he told himself, "perhaps no longer for me, but for her, it still exists." He toppled over full length on the ground, he clutched at the ground with his fingernails. He saw a blinding light, the light of the midsummer fire. He was perched on his father's shoulders, his two hands wrapped around his forehead. He heard his protective voice. "Hide yourself well," said his father, "bury yourself well, my little quail." He was now very far away, at the foot of a great bright wall that he would have to cross in his depth, but Mo ordered him desperately to refuse—she was crying that he must stop, come back. It was an effort and a time without measure.

Right at the end, the pain began to recede, as if being drunk by the earth, with its dry scent that at length he rediscovered near his mouth. Under his fingers, a granular material disintegrated. Later, he could clearly distinguish the flowers, the course of the path, understood that he was returning. He waited a long time, aware of the slight burning sensation on his cheek from the crushed grass blades. Finally, he had the violent desire to sit up, to hold his stick, to get to his feet. He was standing. He still had the bag with the bread swung over his shoulder. A shadow of joy danced around him, light and hesitant, which he felt more and more clearly brush against him, surround him, support him. Leaning heavily on his cane, he took one step, then another. His heart remained nearly calm, he only had to stop often. Finally he opened the little valley door and banged it behind him on all his defeated enemies. At the end of the grassy terrace, under the arbor, Maria and Mo were seated, shelling peas. As soon as she saw him, Mo got up. Once more, there was morning.